The Dragons' Apprentice

a science faction novella for supporters of
co-operatives, social enterprises and the social
and solidarity economy

by

Rory Ridley-Duff

In memoriam - Social Enterprise London,
lest we forget the radical vision of its founders.

 First published in October 2014 by the author to FairShares Association members via *Loomio.org*.

 The author and the FairShares Association publish this novella as a joint project: fifty percent of revenues will be reinvested in FairShares Association activities.

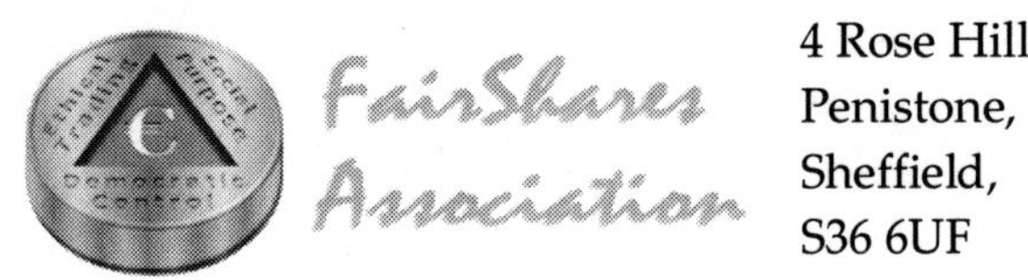

4 Rose Hill Close,
Penistone,
Sheffield,
S36 6UF

---

www.fairshares.coop

Cover images provided by CanStockPhoto, Halifax, Canada

Rory Ridley-Duff

Fast forward to 2032. In a co-operative world full of social enterprises, the BBC hires a new quartet of Dragons…

Warren is an entrepreneur who has successfully amassed billions. Unfortunately, since receiving an ASBO for anti-social investing, he has been banned from starting any new ventures. Then he receives a call from Sharon - an ambitious producer at the BBC – to ask if he would like to put his unemployed capital back to work on a new game show. Should he accept?

I

Welcome to the *Dragons*

Sharon Brook, the producer of *Dragons' Cave,* knocked on Davina's and Adriana's dressing room door.

"Are you ready, ladies?" she shouted.

Davina opened the door.

"You want to come in?" she asked.

"Yeah, it's ten minutes to the live call so I wanted to let you know the running order," said Sharon.

Davina cleared papers from a spare chair to make room for Sharon to sit down.

"Quick drink?" asked Davina.

"Very quick," said Sharon.

Davina had developed a taste for shots of vodka and lime and poured one for Sharon.

"There. Get that down you!" said Davina.

Sharon knocked back the drink in one go and shook her face when the alcohol burned the back of her throat.

"Hi, Sharon," said Adriana, who shared a room with Davina.

Sharon attempted to say 'Hi' back, but the vodka had momentarily stripped her of the ability to speak. She nodded once as an acknowledgment.

"We're all set, I think. You want me to get the guys?" asked Adriana.

Sharon nodded again so Adriana knocked noisily on the plasterboard and bellowed in the direction of the neighbouring dressing room.

"ED! CLIFF! Get your arses in here – Sharon wants to start the show!"

With four children, Adriana had grown accustomed to barking orders at the men in her life and sure enough, it had the right effect. Within 30 seconds, Ed and Cliff appeared at the door.

"So what have we got tonight?" asked Cliff.

Sharon handed Davina, Adriana, Ed and Cliff a piece of paper each.

"First up is Polyana," said Sharon. "She's a bit up tight but trying desperately to hide it."

"What can we expect from her?" asked Ed.

"Not sure," replied Sharon. "She's not sharing her thoughts much and has kept her head down since she got here. Studying you all hard, I think, so you don't surprise her. Diligent, smart, professional."

"Oh Christ," replied Adriana. "Not a 'professional' contestant. They're the worst."

Cliff put his arm around Adriana.

"You'll survive," he comforted before breaking into song. "Because…'you're a survivor…you're not gon give up…you're not gon stop…you're gon work harder!'

Adriana gave Cliff a fake punch in the stomach for reminding her of the signature tune that the BBC had used to promote her appearance on the show. Adriana's life hit a low point twenty years before. It was an infamy that – with the twists of history – propelled her to fame. As a single mother with four children, she found herself on the wrong side of three consecutive redundancy programmes after the hospitals in her area were privatised. After the third, she camped outside parliament with her children to draw attention to her plight. Within weeks, she became the face of the 2018 revolution. The song spoke the truth – she was a survivor.

"And here you are now – an international TV star," said Ed. "Almost as famous as me!"

Of the four, Ed was the Dragon that had the greatest love of the limelight. He was in the final stages of a distinguished career and openly relished the media opportunities that now came his way. He missed the ducking and diving and all the wheeling and dealing that he had needed to survive the fall of capitalism. The media – he found – had its own wheelers and dealers and he felt at home amongst them.

Cliff, however, was a complete contrast. Sharon brought him in to add balance to the panel. Cliff had always been a quiet person, but was revered much more than the other three. Davina, Adriana and Ed were all national heroes, but Cliff was an international star. He could appear on the *Dragons' Cave* anywhere in the world except North America and be instantly recognised by his audience. Ironically, he'd never sought fame. He regarded it as an occupational hazard, not a mark of success. He agreed to appear on the show out of respect for Sharon's skills as a producer. Indeed, Cliff's stature owed much to a documentary that Sharon made about him ten years earlier. He owed her and this was his way of making the repayment.

"Second up is Warren," said Sharon. "He's a bit of an odd-ball if you ask me."

"How so?" asked Davina.

"Normally this lot are cocky and smug. He's not. In fact, I would say he's a bit overwhelmed by it," added Sharon.

"Are you asking us to go gently?" responded Davina.

"No, definitely not," replied Sharon. "Don't get me wrong. He's not short of confidence. It is just that ---"

Sharon paused to recall Warren's background check.

"---he's been out of the game for a long time. Since 2019."

"So it's *that* Warren," commented Cliff with a glint in his eye.

Davina, Adriana and Ed all looked puzzled, but neither Cliff nor Sharon rushed to enlighten them.

"Yes, it's *that* Warren," confirmed Sharon.

Cliff touched his nose to indicate he would not share his knowledge with his fellow panellists.

"And who's the final contestant?" asked Davina.

"One for you," responded Sharon. "He was a big bad union busting employer before he switched careers. In fact, I would say that he's one of the main reasons your profession enjoys such high status."

Davina was a well-known mediator, one of the winners in a profession that had grown inexorably on the back of member-ownership.[1] Mediators regarded people as social equals during the resolution of a dispute. As employers rarely saw themselves as the social equal of their employees, they rarely hired mediators. But member-owners assumed they were equal to their peers. So, as member-ownership became more popular, mediators replaced HR consultants. Owners no longer wanted professional help to sack people, they wanted professional help to keep them.

"And what's his name?" asked Davina, hoping she would know him.

"His name is William," replied Sharon.

Davina shook her head. Sharon saw Cliff touch his nose again to indicate that he might know which William she was referring to.

"Right, you lot," said Sharon assertively. "Let's get you on that stage. I'm hearing that Polyana is in the wings."

"One minute!" shouted someone outside the dressing room. Adriana and Davina got to their feet and followed Ed and Cliff out of the door.

The lights came up. The music started. The show began.

II

Patricia tunes into her favourite programme…

It was one of the world's strangest sights. Patricia Firth – one of the nation's most distinguished legal minds – stood in the middle of her living room in her Moodsy. Her chameleon-like pyjamas changed from red to orange to yellow as she anticipated the start of the *Dragons' Cave.* She kicked off her slippers, picked up a glass of wine in her right hand and gestured to switch on the TV with her left. Her peers, she had no doubt, would be out at high class restaurants, visiting the opera or enjoying a West End show. Five years ago - when her husband was alive - she would probably have been doing the same.

But now, each Saturday night she had a date with prime time TV. Her daughter, Natasha, would arrive a few minutes before 7.30 with a takeaway from the local *FairSlice* outlet. This week they had ordered a 12" pizza called the Vegetable Summit. The vendor's advert boasted of the delightful 'slow rising crust', 'beautiful blend' of mozzarella and blue cheeses, and 'congregation' of red and yellow peppers at its centre.

"I can't stay tonight, mum," said Natasha handing over the piping hot food. "Sharon called me an hour ago and wants me at the studio by 8."

"Well, that's just too bad," said Patricia. "Can you hurry back?"

"I will," she said. "As soon as I can get away."

"All dressed for the occasion?" queried Patricia.

"Well, if I am called onto the stage, I've got to look the part," replied Natasha.

"Okay, run along," she said kissing her daughter on the cheek. "I'll save you some wine."

"Bye, mum," said Natasha. "Enjoy the show!"

"I'll look out for you," said Patricia as she closed the door.

Both mother and daughter had pursued careers in law. Patricia, unlike her daughter, had put all her energies into law enforcement. Patricia disagreed with her daughter's views on the rule of law – she still believed it was the bedrock of a civilized society. Without being naïve about its shortcomings, she remained confident that it prevented populist zealots and potential dictators from taking power. And a judiciary independent of the government was still the best way to guarantee freedoms that citizens took for granted (or aspired to have).

Her daughter took a different view. Natasha felt that the revolution in 2018 was necessary to curb corruption of the law-making process. She believed that social progress had slowed in the late 20th century, then stopped completely after the Millennium. It resumed only when social movements started to subvert the law. They took what had been written to protect the rich and used it to protect the poor. Natasha respected her mother, but did not want to be her protégé.

But they did share a passion for the *Dragons' Cave.* It was one thing that bound them together in a way that blood relations and the legal profession could not. As Natasha headed enthusiastically to the TV studio, Patricia settled on the sofa and raised her glass to the Dragons. They walked boldly to their chairs, illuminated by a fanfare of light, greeted by familiar jingles. A narrator's voice gave a quick overview of the show's format and briefed the audience on what to expect.

Patricia became addicted to the show because people she met professionally appeared on it regularly. She knew them particularly well because it was her professional duty to discern the smallest details of their lives and apply the law correctly to them. These were complicated people, not only used to getting their way by virtue of their wealth, but also willing and able to squeeze through the smallest legal cracks left open by colluding politicians.

"I remember you," she exclaimed as Polyana walked onto the stage. "What a slippery creature you are – always armed with three lawyers to spoil my day!"

She sipped a glass of Chablis while the Dragons' proceeded to quiz Polyana. It was not long before Ed was shaking his head. For a while, Polyana seemed to make headway with Adriana and Davina but eventually they too raised their hands to end the conversation. So, it all came down to Cliff. Could Polyana persuade Cliff to accept the deal that she was offering?

Patricia's interest had a macabre quality. So far as she knew, none of her colleagues watched the show. But to her, it was a fascinating critique of the so-called Dark Age from which they had emerged. Institutions that she had taken for granted during her upbringing had been turned on their head. It was the changes that inclined her daughter to follow a different path, to become a pioneer of a different approach to justice.

"Come on, Cliff," shouted Patricia at the TV. "If anyone can control this wily wretch, it's you!"

Cliff was Patricia's favourite Dragon. He was about her age and they had met socially a few times. In truth, she had a bit of a crush on him and seeing him every Saturday night fuelled her desire to renew his acquaintance. Patricia had tried (in vain) to get Natasha to bring Cliff home after the show. Her daughter insisted that it was 'not that kind of relationship'. Even so, Patricia sensed that Natasha and Cliff were close. She always seemed to be hatching ideas with him and when the call from Sharon came earlier in the evening, Patricia assumed that something significant was going to happen on the show.

Whatever it was, however, would not involve Polyana. She had failed in her pitch to Cliff and was now talking to the show's host. He thanked her for applying, commiserated with her for not closing a deal, and then turned to look at the camera. With his face in close up, a ritual began that ended with the first commercial break. As the words 'Cut!' echoed in the earpieces of the stage crew, Patricia was already making herself a mug of coffee.

III

Warren waits in the wings…

"Are you nervous?" asked Sharon.

"Yes," replied Warren, simply.

Sharon had taken a keen interest in Warren, much more so than the other contestants. Most of the people she recruited had a lingering anger combined with cocky arrogance. The latter came from the sumptuous lifestyles they enjoyed up to 2018. The former was rooted in their sense of betrayal by the legal system. Prior to 2018, it had protected them, but now it had abandoned them to shows like this.

But Warren was different. Unlike Polyana who still power-dressed to negotiate her deal, Warren had chosen to dress casually. He looked like he was on his way to meet friends in a London bar, while she looked like she was returning from a G8 summit. When Warren was cocky, Sharon felt it was a performance that served a purpose. Polyana and William, on the other hand, seemed to ooze arrogance from every pore of their bodies all the time.

"You'll be fine," said Sharon.

Warren acknowledged her comment and made small talk.

"Have you run this show for long?" he asked.

"Three years," she replied.

"Is it fun?"

Sharon smiled.

"Yes. It's been fun."

"Can't imagine this being fun for the contestants," added Warren.

"Want to pull out?" Sharon probed.

Warren studied Sharon. He guessed that she was a little younger than himself and looked after herself by running or attending the gym. He liked her dress sense which was smart without being formal. He could not see any sign that she had children or was married. Her left wrist supported a tasteful ethnic bracelet which he guessed she had chosen for herself. Her feet were adorned by stylish leather boots that matched a pair of brown slacks. Her blouse was snug in all the right places and it completed an image that yielded a pleasant aura. Warren wondered if the woman inside was as agreeable as her outfit.

"I wouldn't let you down like that, Sharon."

"You'll be fine," I promise. "I've not seen the Dragons' eat any of the contestants yet," she reassured.

"Not physically," commented Warren. "But I have seen some get a good mauling."

Sharon realised that platitudes would not satisfy him.

"It happens, but mainly to people who under-estimate the Dragons," she replied.

"Any words of wisdom?" asked Warren.

"Roll with the punches," she said, with the air of a woman who had seen a few onscreen fights.

"Thanks," he said with a smile.

Sharon's phone rang.

"Yep," she said in a clipped tone. "Hi! Where are you?"

Sharon nodded.

"Okay, see you in a few minutes. Bye."

"Anything interesting?" asked Warren.

"That's your date for after the show," replied Sharon.

"Didn't know I had one," he replied.

"We know how to look after our guests," Sharon replied pleasantly.

"I can hardly wait," answered Warren, intrigued.

Sharon and Warren watched as the Dragons returned to their chairs. When the lights came up, the stage crew knew that the commercial break would end in 30 seconds. The narrator got ready to introduce Warren.

Sharon took Warren's arm and led him to the edge of the stage.

"Come back in one piece," she said.

"Wish me luck?" he asked.

Sharon showed him that the fingers of her right hand were crossed, then gave him a gentle shove with her left hand. Warren walked across the stage giving out a smile to mask his fear of the mauling he fully expected to get.

IV

Warren enters the *Dragons' Cave*...

The four Dragons huddled together in a row waiting for the next candidate to arrive. They were discussing the unimaginative offer they had just received, and were now hoping that the next contestant would have more up-to-date knowledge of investing.

"Here he comes," commented Cliff. "He's not overdressed, at least."

Cliff was the most seasoned of the Dragons, a veteran warrior who had toured the globe with ideas and won the hearts and minds of people across Asia and Africa. More recently, his ideas had found favour in Europe and he was now a celebrity. In retirement, he contented himself with these occasional appearances on the British Broadcasting Co-operative.[2]

"Let's hope he's better than the last one. Shocking presentation! Shocking offer," said Ed.

Adriana and Davina chuckled, remembering crass and ludicrous statements made by the last candidate. It was obvious she'd never seen the inside of a co-operative business school, or even a co-operative for that matter.

Draped in the aura of legitimacy that comes from being repeatedly elected by work colleagues to positions of influence, the Dragons waited to see what the new candidate had to say. Warren walked onto the TV set, looking as nervous as he felt intimidated.

"Good morning, Dragons", said Warren politely. "I've looked carefully at your four businesses, and I'd like to focus on Ed's, if I may."

"Social enterprises, Warren," corrected Ed. "Social enterprises, not businesses." Ed hated it when people used such archaic and imprecise words.[3]

Ed was the elected chair of *miMarket*, one of the UK's highly regarded solidarity co-operatives.[4] His social enterprise was now 20 years old, one of a new generation of retail empires that had decided to split equity and dividends 50/50 between workforce and consumer members. He was a seasoned professional with 14 years of experience organising community share issues. It never ceased to amaze him how investors were still living in the Dark Age. This time, he was hoping for a sensible offer.

Warren got out his investment wallet and cheque iPad. A bead of sweat started to roll down his right temple.

"My analysis, Ed, is that your business - sorry, social enterprise - is under-capitalised. I'd like to invest a billion euros in return for a 30% equity stake."

The four Dragons laughed but Warren did not understand what he had said to amuse them. Ed settled back into his chair before addressing Warren.

"What's that in MPMs?" he asked.[5]

"Mobile phone minutes? At today's conversion rate... ....about 330 million."

"Thank you," said Ed, politely. "Do you know anything about how my enterprise is structured?" he continued.

Warren did not so he chose to remain quiet.

"You do understand what type of enterprise I've been elected to chair?" Ed repeated, with a small emphasis on the word 'elected'.

"Erm," said Warren nervously. "I think so, Ed. You're a co-operative."

"Yes that's right," responded Ed.

Warren's confidence momentarily increased. "I've been looking at your balance sheet," he continued, "and it says that you've got about..." Warren paused as he did the calculation to mobile phone minutes in his head.

"...1 billion MPMs in share capital. Your sales are so strong on the international market that I think you are going to need more working capital for your localisation plans. But obviously, there's a risk involved, so I'd want 30% of your business."

Ed smiled and let the *faux pas* go uncorrected. Habits were clearly hard to break for those still living in the Dark Age.

"You seem to be confusing us with the Co-operative Bank," said Ed dismissively. "What exactly do you know about modern solidarity co-ops, Warren?"

Ed had to keep a straight face for the cameras, but inside he found it hard to stop laughing. He could see that Cliff, Adriana and Davina were all smirking. This would be excellent TV for the viewers, waiting in anticipation for the humbling, the moment of deep embarrassment.

Warren shuffled uneasily. What had he done wrong? Why was Ed looking so strangely at him?

Ed continued to play to the camera for the benefit of the audience.

"Warren," he said earnestly. "What did you learn about solidarity co-ops when you studied 'business'?"

"Nothing," he replied. Warren had been to college in the years leading up to 2018 when the hubris of business schools had been so great that they had ignored co-operative and social enterprise values and principles. "I just studied business, Ed," continued Warren.

In the privacy of his own mind, Warren recalled a series of reforms at the Co-operative Group.[6] Like many, Warren was confused that it was allowed to keep using this name after it ceased to be a co-operative. Warren remembered the fanfare when it listed on the London Stock Exchange and seemed to become the same as any other business he had invested in. And yet, he was sure the murmur cascading around the audience like a Mexican wave had a meaning that he had not grasped.

"No, Warren," contradicted Ed, "you just studied *private* business. Well, now you need to know about new co-operativism and social enterprise. You can't come to an event like this without doing your research. You can't come here and expect the Dragons to take you seriously if you don't understand mainstream models. Do you know how social value is created? Can you describe sustainable development to me? Can you read an SROI statement? Can you explain where the co-operative advantage comes from?"

Warren did not know where to look. Adriana felt sorry for him and she hated this pompous and judgemental side of Ed's character. It was not Warren's fault he was so ignorant: it was the way he had been brought up! She tried to put Warren out of his misery.

"Warren. What Ed means to say is that you can't buy equity in his co-operative."[7]

"Why's that?" asked Warren, deciding to play dumb so he did not look any more foolish.

Davina could not contain herself any longer.

"Because you're an investor," she said, as if it was the most obvious thing in the world. "Investors can't own equity. Only workers and customers can do that."[8]

"What?" said Warren, who still clung to the distant memory of his father as one of the world's top investors. He so wanted to make a political speech about the wonders of private enterprise. "You mean I actually have to do some work before I can invest?"

"Yes, of course," said Davina. "Or be a regular customer. What on earth are you thinking? You can't just give a co-op money and expect to take its profits without participating in its operation."

Warren looked perplexed. That was what he had done all his life until his capital had been reclassified as unemployed in 2018. Now he had to live off his investments without being able to make any new ones. It felt like purgatory. His friends complained endlessly about the social economy because billions of working people in all parts of the world had abandoned private banks and chosen to put their money into credit unions. Now there was an endless stream of competitive loans from democratically controlled financial institutions. The private banks had a dwindling base of customers willing to pay extortionate rates of interest.

Warren felt that he had to know more so he responded positively when the BBC called him and asked if he would participate in a programme to put unemployed capital back to work. He thought God was smiling on him and his fortunes were about to change. This was his chance. At last, his capital might be employed again. His nightmare would be over.

"Go back to co-op school," said Adriana, conscious of Warren's need to improve his education. "You need to understand what you're dealing with."

Adriana said this to him as kindly as possible, but underneath she felt sorry for him. Since the silent revolution, most investors had been cut loose by the market. They wandered around, clustered on street corners, moaning about their unemployed capital. After the switch to MPMs as a global currency, nobody wanted their dollars, euros and pounds any more, and it left them feeling depressed and hollow. Life made no sense. It was meaningless. Many turned to petty crimes like gambling in casinos and buying scratch cards. Some desperate souls (realising they could not even give their capital away) felt suicidal. The Samaritans had reported a 500% increase in calls from City investors over the last 10 years.

"So what must I do?" said Warren, crestfallen.

"We do pay fixed interest to investors who give us loans," said Davina.

Davina did this to help Ed who she knew was the keenest to help investors out of work poverty. Davina's employer *The National Co-operative of Mediators* had replaced the *Employment Tribunal Service* after disciplinary and grievance rules had been scrapped in 2020. She preferred to raise capital solely through community share issues. Ed, on the other hand, was prepared to adopt a mixed approach and accept loans from outside investors and pay them a small rate of interest.

"At what rate?" asked Warren, hopefully.

"At the current bank base rate plus 2%," said Ed.

"So I'd get only 2.5%?" asked Warren. In times past, he had sometimes achieved a 20% return in a week when short-selling a national economy. This was madness. This was hell on earth. This was a nightmare.

"Yes, 2.5% at the moment. It's not our fault you destroyed the banking system. You brought it on yourselves, you know," said Ed with bitterness as he remembered losing his life savings in the crash of 2008.

"You could do some voluntary work," suggested Cliff, who had been staying quiet and biding his time. "We can't arrange a job until you've had a co-operative education, but voluntary work would be a start."

"Voluntary work?" asked Warren, even more perplexed.

"Yes, you could keep all your money and just invest your labour," suggested Cliff, maintaining his poker face.

"You mean, I work for you and get no ROI at all?" This seemed like the stupidest suggestion Warren had ever heard in his life.

"That's the pot calling the kettle black," whispered Adriana to Davina as she recalled the three times she had been made redundant during the NHS 'reforms' of 2013-18. Now she was the proud co-owner of *Better Health*,[9] the country's most respected designer of clinics and community hospitals. She was the only member of the workforce to have been elected three times to its parliament.

"You'll create some social capital," said Cliff with positivity that he knew the audience would appreciate.

At this suggestion, Ed felt he had to step in.

"Shame on you, Cliff, for suggesting that we don't pursue a double-bottom line for Warren," he said as he winked at Cliff out of camera shot.

"Warren," he said, turning his attention to the increasingly bemused investor, "you obviously need a guiding hand to get back into investing. What you need is a mentor, and I think we can help you with that. How about we discuss how many of your euros we can convert to an MPM loan, and you also come to do some voluntary work for me as well?"

Warren started to feel desperate, and despite not wanting to work, he needed a chance to feel whole again by making a new financial investment.

"Would either of you take my money at 3%?" he said, looking hopefully at Adriana and Davina.

"I'm out," said Davina, cutting Warren off immediately.

"Too steep for me!" said Adriana.

"You drive a hard bargain, Warren," said Ed. "For 3%, I'll not just want some of your euros and some voluntary work, I'd also want some free advertising in your media empire and to fund your education at the Co-operative University."

Warren had always hated his media empire but it had made him a lot of money. He found it ironic that he kept it given his grandfather's reclusive lifestyle. The offer of a university education seemed attractive, however. His father had always told him that he did not need one, seeing as he was so rich. Things were different now. Completing his education would surely come in handy. Luckily they had not forced investors to give up their fortunes in 2018 so he still had a chance to make a new life. Warren thought about the 3% return on investment – it was a bad deal, but at least some of his capital could get back to work. It was hopelessly one-sided, but the best he was likely to get.

Ed could see that Warren was still hesitating.

"If your work and studies go well," said Ed, "you might even become a full member."

"And would I then be able to buy equity?" asked Warren.

"Non-transferable co-operative equity," replied Ed.

That was good enough for Warren. It would diversify his portfolio.

"Deal," he quickly announced and shook Ed's hand, hiding his resentment as best he could.

The camerawoman zoomed in to catch the apparent pleasure on both their faces while the music for the commercial break began to play. After a few more seconds, the producer, Sharon Brook whispered 'Cut!' into the ear-piece of the camerawoman. "Okay everyone, take 15 minutes while we prepare for the next investor," she shouted.

Cliff smiled. He had worked all his life for a world in which labour hired capital rather than the other way around. This was heaven. This was justice. It was cruel justice at times, but justice nevertheless. And it was excellent edutainment. As the floor assistant brought him his customary fair-trade coffee, he let his mind wander back to 2012, the year that the United Nations in an act of wisdom that surprised most of his peers, decided to sponsor the International Year of Co-operatives. That was when it had really got going. That was when his boat started to come in.

In 2012, there was a powerful but silent revolution. Following the *Occupy Wall Street* protests (in which financial districts were taken over by millions of people), technologies for participatory democracy emerged rapidly. There was: *loomio.org* for online conferencing and decision-making; *co-budget* for collaborative co-operative budgeting; *crowdfunder.co.uk* and *kickstarter.com* for philanthropic funding, *zopa.com* and *microgenius.org.uk* for mutual lending, borrowing and community shares, and then *crowdcube.com* and *fundingcircle.com* for small scale investments in start-up companies.[10] Within 5 years, people were questioning whether company boards, chief financial officers and investment managers were necessary – most of their professional skills has been coded into IT systems that were transparent and democratic. It put small investors in charge of their portfolio without fund managers creaming off fees each year.

Governments eventually had to respond too. They devised strategies to pay off national debts by raising taxes on speculative share trading and charging fees for digital money. But even that was not sufficient to quell the accumulation of grievances felt by the populace. In 2019, the *Members Direct* organisation[11] – in which Cliff played a large role – organised the takeover of *Facebook* and *LinkedIn* through a mutual buyout of private owners. Its members quickly voted to end all cooperation with state surveillance authorities to restore freedom of association, speech and thought.

By 2025, most social networks across the global had converted themselves into a mutual or co-operative society. The key year was generally regarded as 2018 when western governments became so afraid for their own futures that they passed laws to make stock broking a criminal offence. By 2030, social democratic values had reshaped laws on enterprise ownership and a new human right – the right to co-own your workplace – was extended to every person of working age.

There was resistance, of course, with private employers ignoring workers' new rights. Harold Porter, a politician in the New Conservative Party, organised opposition and lobbied for the restoration of corporate rights to private property. In the new Human Rights Charter, the property rights of legal persons were restricted and the word 'personal' had replaced 'private' to distinguish the rights of corporations from the rights of natural persons.[12]

Social networks organised campaigns to identify employers who ignored human rights. Members collaborated to identify recalcitrant employers and predatory investors. They passed evidence to new citizen courts that had new powers to issue anti-social behaviour orders (ASBOs)[13] to limit an employer's or investor's power to make investments until they complied with the law.

University lecturers started to distribute case studies of Enron, Worldcom and the financial crashes of 1997, 2001, 2008 and 2012 to teach students about the demise of private enterprise. Histories of *Facebook* and *LinkedIn* became required reading in a new core curriculum on Participatory Democracy (alongside Maths and English).

* * *

Cliff's thoughts were interrupted by the sight of two people dressed in black. It was a policeman and woman who were greeted by Sharon Brook. They looked towards Ed and Warren, gesturing in their direction, then made their way across the stage. The policewoman, Natasha, walked up to Warren.

"Mr Buffet Junior?" she asked.

"Yes," Warren answered.

"The TV station just received a call from a viewer. They claim that you've broken the terms of your ASBO by attempting to make an investment. Please come with me."

Warren looked bewildered as Natasha escorted him from the TV set. His nightmare was not over. In fact, it was about to get worse.

V

Arrested on the set of the *Dragons' Cave*, Warren crosses The Thin Blue Line…

Warren huddled in the back of the police car. He sat uncomfortably between Sharon, the *Dragons' Cave* producer who insisted on accompanying them to the station, and Officer Natasha who had arrested him.

"I'm so sorry," said Sharon. "I don't understand why our researchers didn't spot this when they prepared for the show. I'd never have put you on if I'd known you had an ASBO!"

The law on anti-social behaviour orders - ASBOs for short - had been reformed after the revolution of 2018, and again in 2030 during the second Police Reform Act. It now extended to investors who had put their money into activities 'harmful to human well-being'. Predatory investors – of which Warren was one – received ASBOs banning them from making any new investments.

"Let's wait and see what Warren's got to say for himself down the station, shall we?" said Natasha, who felt considerably less sympathetic.

"I want to stay with him," Sharon insisted.

Until convicted, the new Police Reform Act gave a person the right to be accompanied by a friend, colleague or relative (in addition to a lawyer) whenever in the presence of law enforcement officers.

Warren was taken aback. Why would she do that? He was nothing to her. She was nothing to him.

"As long as that's alright with you?" Sharon asked Warren, sensing his discomfort.

Warren nodded. Natasha acknowledged Sharon's request and phoned ahead to make the arrangements.

The police car in which they travelled was light blue. The Old Bill had been gradually transformed after the revelations that came to light during the Leveson Inquiry.[14] In 2013, it published its report and revealed the scale of corruption involving press barons and police officers, and a hidden industry of private investigators who corrupted police services to access information that corporations used to intimidate citizens and politicians who challenged their interests. The Thin Blue Line had become too thin so civil society organisations started to pilot new constabularies[15] with officers directly accountable through a new social enterprise called Citizen Opinion. It went national in 2018 and acted swiftly to secure the first Police Reform Act. Police officers were now required to attend mediation if their law enforcement activities harmed a third party not involved in unlawful activity. The Local Bill – as they became known – replaced The Old Bill. Natasha was one of its high profile media liaison officers, with special powers to develop new innovations in the rehabilitation of offenders.

Citizen Opinion was not the first mutual enterprise to give people a voice in shaping institutions that dominate their lives. The first was *patientopinion.org.uk*, a venture that transformed NHS services by publishing detailed accounts of patient care.[16] The second was Employee Opinion - a joint venture with the TUC - that countered corporate power by publishing case studies of working conditions. Citizen Opinion was the third. It was established in 2016 to allow members of the public to share their experiences of the justice system. In all three projects, positive and negative accounts created a rich, balanced and dynamic knowledge base for improving practice.

* * *

Within thirty minutes, Sharon and Warren were sitting in a police interview room awaiting his lawyer. As breaking an ASBO was a contempt of court, he faced a possible jail term.

"Why are you here?" asked Warren, unable to contain his curiosity.

"What?" responded Sharon, perplexed.

"Why are you here?" repeated Warren. "It's a simple enough question."

"I didn't like the way the Dragons talked to you," she said.

"Isn't humiliating people like me the point of the show?" he asked.

"Absolutely not," Sharon responded. "It's to confront the reckless system your generation created and to learn about alternatives people are creating for themselves."

"And what are they, exactly?"

"Did you learn nothing from the show?" asked Sharon.

"I learnt that the Dragons are as pompous and arrogant as they were 25 years ago."

"Nothing else?" she added.

"And that they are as pompous and arrogant as I am," he added without any hint he was joking.

Sharon laughed.

"So you are capable of self-reflection, then?" she said pointedly.

"I've always known I'm pompous and arrogant," he said, this time with a trace of a smile.

"Not traits you revealed on the show," she commented.

"I don't believe in traits," he revealed. "I think my behaviour is an outcome of character meeting context."

Sharon was surprised. She had not imagined he would hold such an Owenite perspective on human nature.[17]

"So, you're a closet socialist and believe we're all products of our environment?" she asked.

"Not at all," Warren replied. "I've just seen too many hard-working entrepreneurs become corrupt after I put money into their businesses."

"Maybe you bring out the worst in them?" Sharon queried.

"So, why *are* you here?" he asked again, "because if you're just going to insult me, I'd prefer you to piss off."

Sharon paused. Warren said this flippantly rather than angrily so she wondered if she should be more open with him. As a producer, despite the freedoms that came with the role, there was a need to hold something in reserve. However, it had not been a spur of the moment choice to jump in the car with Officer Natasha. It gave Sharon a chance to study Warren closely and see if he was suitable.

"I like you," she said.

"You've a funny way of showing it," Warren responded, pleasantly surprised by her comment.

"You don't bullshit. You don't pretend. And I don't believe you are as pompous and arrogant as you say you are," she insisted.

Warren became a bit suspicious.

"So is it my money?" he probed.

"Fuck your money," she replied with a smile.

"Now that I'd like to see," he said.

Adopting a more mischievous tone, Sharon replied.

"Let's see what unfolds, shall we?"

Warren felt a rush of adrenalin. Was she flirting? Clearly, she was not there just because of the encounter with the Dragons. He sensed there was something more and he wanted to know what it was.

"So, what is this 'social enterprise' thing Ed kept talking about?" he asked.

"Didn't you learn anything from the *Dragons' Cave*?" she asked, searchingly.

"I learnt that social enterprises are shit investment opportunities, run by people who are more popular than intelligent, and that will only give me a 2 – 3% return on my money."

"Wrong on all counts," she replied. She realised it would be fruitless to engage him in any discussion about 'social returns'.

"So tell me!" he exclaimed. All the time, he was searching in his mind for a way to establish her motive for accompanying him to the police station.

"You want me to define social enterprises for you?" she asked.

"Why not, if they're so great? What d'you see in them?"

"The motives behind them," she replied, "and the human values created by them."

"Sentimental rubbish," Warren intervened. "We had charity types in my companies. Never made any difference in the long run."

"But it does now," insisted Sharon. "It makes all the difference in the world."

"Charity sucks," replied Warren.

"Perhaps your business values suck?" questioned Sharon. "And where d'you get the idea that social enterprise is charity?" she added forcefully.

"Are you saying it's not?"

"Not usually. It can be something charities do, but it's conceptually different."

"So - it's not business, it's not charity, and we can safely say it's not public sector?"

Sharon nodded.

"But you *still* can't tell me what it is," he taunted.

Sharon looked at Warren more closely. How could 30 years of debate about social economy have by-passed him? What had cocooned him from the changes that had followed the revolution?

"I just can't believe that I have to," she responded eventually.

"Private enterprise will rise again, one day, you'll see," taunted Warren.

"You really think so?" she replied, inquisitively.

Warren did not actually believe this and it showed. Things had gone too far. The robustness and stability of the economy since 2018 was obvious to him and his friends. The EU laws giving governments control over the creation of digital money gave them effective power over private banks. For the first time in living memory, private bank bosses had to develop a profound respect for local democratic assemblies and parliaments. Warren's strategy of goading her into revealing her passion for social enterprise was not working. She just kept asking questions that he did not want to answer.

"Have you ever invested in trading activity where human well-being was central to the enterprise's purpose and design?" she asked.

"Lots of people benefitted from my investing, not least those who got jobs," he replied.

"That's not the question I asked," she corrected. "Have you invested in trading activity that has the well-being of people as central?"

Warren, schooled by his father to 'avoid do-gooders', had still made some strategic charity donations.

"I've given to charities," he said defensively.

"That's **not** the question," Sharon repeated. "When have you made investing in the well-being of people *central* to your investment decisions?"

Warren tried to think. He had made money from Monsanto, but since finding out the impact of their drugs he was not convinced they advanced 'well-being'. He had supported agri-businesses, but so many farmers had been poisoned by chemicals or left dependant on genetically engineered seed (to the benefit of the seed maker) that he did not regard that as 'well-being' either. Then a thought came into his head.

"I once invested in renewable energy," he proudly announced.

"Who benefitted from that?" Sharon asked.

"Well…the environment, obviously! Then the farmers on whose land we built the turbines," he added.

"Who owned the enterprise? How were its profits shared out or reinvested?" Sharon asked.

Warren threw his hands up. He could not remember. He did remember that he got a good return on his investment for a while, but he put that down to the government subsidies that were available at the time. When he got advance warning that subsidies would be withdrawn, he sold his shares.

Warren shrugged his shoulders.

"Why make me work so hard?" he complained. "Just tell me."

"I've already told you," she said.

"No you haven't," he argued.

"Yes, I have. Three times…"

"What?" Warren aped Sharon's style of talking. "So it's a business that puts the well-being of people at the heart of its investment decisions?"

"Close enough," Sharon said. "It requires the well-being of the workforce, customers and wider environment to be central, not marginal, when making decisions."

"No different to *private* enterprise," Warren asserted confidently.

"News International's phone hacking? Union Carbide at Bhopal? Enron's energy businesses? BP's gulf oil spill? G4S's failure to police the Olympics? Serco's claiming for non-existent prisoners? Foxconn's employee suicides? Monsanto's milk production hormones? Bechtel's water privatisation schemes? Big banks' insurance mis-selling scandals?" she retorted. "Were the interests of workforces, customers and the environment considered?"

Warren remained silent.

"So I think there are three distinctive qualities that identify social enterprises," added Sharon. "1. Social purpose and impact. 2. Sustainable, ethical production and consumption. 3. Wealth sharing arrangements that are controlled by democratic assemblies of producers and customers."[18]

"Oh, so now we're back to 'co-operative principles' are we?"

So, he *had* been listening, thought Sharon. She nodded to affirm his observation.

"And you don't think I'm capable of participating in that?" challenged Warren.

"Do you remember a show called *The Apprentice*?" asked Sharon, deciding to change the subject.

"Yes," answered Warren, with a slight hesitation.

"How do you feel about a role in a new series?

"You want me to be the new Alan Sugar?" asked Warren, dumbfounded.

"No – you idiot," she said playfully without a trace of mockery. "I want you to be a contestant!"

So, *that* was her motive – a new TV show.

"Is *Dragons' Cave* losing the ratings war?" he quipped.

"Just thinking of the future," she reassured.

"So how would it work?" he asked.

"You're good with finance, right?"

"I was," he replied, "before I was made an outlaw."

"Well, the contestants will be competing to get viewers to invest in an enterprise..."

"By doing what?" he asked.

"Designing ways to maximise wealth sharing," she answered.

"Let me guess....in businesses that make well-being central to their investment decisions?"

"Clever lad," she chided. "Think of it as a chance to find a useful role in society."

Warren pondered. Would other investors with ASBOs be competing against him? That might be fun.

"You did know I had an ASBO, didn't you?" he quizzed.

Sharon smiled and nodded.

"Did you set this up?"

Sharon evaded his question.

"Are you *interested*?" she said in a tone that demanded an answer.

"That could work," he chirped enthusiastically. "There's just one problem…"

"What's that?" asked Sharon.

"You'll have to get me out of here first. I really don't fancy a stint in jail."

Sharon got up, walked to the door and pressed a buzzer. Natasha opened the door. Her role as a community liaison officer enabled her to visit the BBC frequently. She knew Sharon well and worked with her on creative ways to rehabilitate difficult troubled citizens.

"Officer Natasha," said Sharon sternly, "did you call *The Dragons' Cave* to alert me about Warren's ASBO?"

"Yes I did," Natasha replied.

"And do you think your constabulary will be pressing charges?"

"That depends," she replied.

"On what?" asked Sharon.

"On whether he'll do *Apprentices*," she smiled.

Both Natasha and Sharon turned to face Warren. As he began to contemplate this turn of events, he felt a surge of energy ignite his body.

"Officer," he said. "You've got me bang to rights. I confess my sins. I throw myself on the mercy of the court. Please let me make a new start.....please let me be a contestant on *Apprentices*."

VI

Arrested on the set of the *Dragons' Cave*, Warren becomes an *Apprentice*…

Peter Dimbleby - like his grandfather – had secured the Chair of the BBC's premier political talk show - *Question Hour*. This week his guests included Sharon Brook producer of the *Dragon's Cave*. Following the death of Alan Sugar in 2028, she persuaded the BBC to recreate another old show with a format that reflected changes in the UK's enterprise culture. To the dismay of the old plutocracy, *Apprentices* secured the number one spot in the TV ratings, prompting the need for Sharon to defend it on business and political programmes.

"And can we have our next question, please, from Harold Porter?" Peter asked.

Harold braced himself. A business owner turned politician, his firm was declared insolvent after the Share Dealing and Securities Act became law. In the public mind, the 24/7 system of share-dealing had been the primary source of financial and political instability. Starting in 2019, new laws were introduced to curb speculative investment. They required companies to declare the dates on which their shares would be available for trading. With the exception of public offers, investors were restricted to trading each company's shares on a few days each year.[19]

Banning share-dealing completely had proved impractical, but radically scaling it down found favour with both the public and beleaguered executives tired of servicing the whims of hedge fund managers. A second bill tightened the laws further in April 2025. This linked trading days to regulatory requirements for filing accounts: shares could only be traded on the 30th working day after a plc's quarterly statement, and on the 60th working day after the filing of a limited company's audited accounts. Executives and directors were no longer allowed to choose the date on which shares were traded.

Harold was bitter. He led campaigns against the legislation and was jailed for his involvement in black market stockbroking. After serving a three-year sentence, he remained unrepentant and quickly picked up two ASBOs: one prevented him from buying or selling stocks in any company; the second banned him from holding a directorship in any firm related to financial services. His right to protest, however, was unimpaired and he had become a politician with a large right-wing following. He campaigned tirelessly against *Apprentices*.

"Do panel members agree that *Apprentices* is brainwashing the show's contestants?"

A few claps were overshadowed by disapproving mutters. Harold had few friends outside the City.

"Sharon," answered Peter with some glee, "I think that's one for you."

"Can Harold clarify, please? The question is absurd," she replied.

Sharon knew Harold and the question well. The Head of BBC programming had put it to her when she proposed the show. *Apprentices* recruited contestants who had received ASBOs for investment activity 'harmful to human well-being' and enrolled them on a social and sustainable enterprise management course. Harold saw this as 'brainwashing'.

"The show's making political prisoners of the participants, turning them into performing monkeys for the public, devaluing their knowledge. It's the modern equivalent of a show trial."

Sharon laughed and launched her defence.

"A 'show trial' – that's a bit *extreme,*" she said, choosing her language to implant the idea that the questioner was an 'extremist'. "Have you disapproved of 'rehabilitation' in the past?" she asked Harold.

He was not ready to answer and his hesitation gave Sharon the chance to put a second question.

"Was the 'rehabilitation' of past criminals also 'brainwashing'?" she asked.

Harold dealt with the questions though an evasion.

"Don't give me a politician's answer," he responded.

"Don't ask me a politician's question," she replied, drawing laughter from the studio audience.

Sharon relented. She held up her hands to indicate that she would answer.

"Okay. Nobody is forced to take part in *Apprentices,*" she started. "We have a problem in our society. We have outlawed the activities of Harold's old firm - that's why he's here tonight attacking *Apprentices*. For twenty years we've let the problem grow of men and women in their middle years pushed to the margins. But this group is different. Harold's not starving. He's got food and a nice home. He even kept much of the money he made. But he, like many others, have been shunned at work and denied a meaningful life. And this is true of about two hundred thousand others affected by the changes. We cut share trading by 90% and people like Harold who previously depended on casino capitalism now have to find work…or go into politics!"

Applause and a few giggles spluttered from parts of the auditorium. Sharon, however, was not finished.

"Suicides used to be highest amongst young men between the ages of 16 – 24, especially war veterans and prison inmates. Today, the highest suicide rates are amongst former stockbrokers."[20]

Harold raised his hand, trying to interrupt, but Peter Dimbleby ignored him.

"*Apprentices* is not about money," Sharon continued. "It is about human transformation. Contestants come back to life when they find new ways to use their skills. We're using - not wasting - their talents."

Harold finally got his chance to intervene and made the most of it.

"If you really wanted to improve their health, repeal the legislation that made them outlaws."

"What about *our* health?" someone in the audience shouted. Unperturbed, Harold continued.

"They were wealth *creators*!" he asserted.

Sharon felt the hairs on her neck bristle.

"They were wealth *destroyers*," she responded sharply.[21]

Peter Dimbleby held up a hand to stop Sharon. He opened up the debate to the other panellists.

"What do you all think?" he interjected.

The panellists – comprising MPs from the Tory, Labour, Liberal-Democrat, Green, Socialist and New Co-operative parties – shaped a new political landscape. The public now wanted participatory democracy, not parliamentary democracy, but dismantling parliament was even harder than reforming the City of London.

The Leveson report, revised in 2013, created a consensus that politicians had been irretrievably corrupted by corporate interests. Avaaz coordinated a global campaign for *electorates* to be able to vote on legislative proposals, rather than politicians. In 2018, the UK became the first country to begin full conversion to a participatory democracy. By 2030, the Social Democracy Act established frameworks for people in Wales, Northern Ireland and England to vote for each and every Act of Parliament.

MPs, fearing a public rebellion, had restructured the social contract. They were now busier (and happier) than ever, working with civil servants to draft laws, facilitating TV and public debates, visiting constituents to take questions and comments, and actively charged with limiting the power of lobbyists. The patronage of party leaders was a thing of the past because the state's role had changed to one of enabling citizens to examine legislative proposals through thousands of public fora. Internet referenda cut costs to a tiny fraction of the level they had been a generation before.[22]

"I find *Apprentices* vulgar," said the Tory MP, "but not without merit. I agree with Sharon that we can't ignore the suicide rates but I'm not sure this show brings investors 'back to life'. It seems more like a deeper and more permanent death!"

At the previous week's meeting of the 1922 Committee, she had argued that all forms of public voting were 'vulgar'. The plebs, she argued - despite sustained improvements in their well-being and literacy following the renationalisation of health and education systems - were still too stupid to participate in politics.[23]

The Socialist MP quickly interjected.

"This show's ratings suggest that the public are still hungry for an alternative to the catastrophic economic management of old. The public understands that 'austerity cuts' were part of a class war to preserve the power of the wealthy. *Apprentices* shows people coming to terms with their past and gives them a chance to redeem themselves. I support the show 100%."

Actually, the Socialist MP did not support the show 100%. Privately, he was on record saying that he would not lose any sleep if contestants were lined up and shot. However, he was no keener to express this view on the BBC than the Tory to state her views on the stupidity of the plebs.

The Green and Labour MPs also argued with each other.

"The show is laudable, but where is the attempt to slow down economic growth?" said the Green.[24]

The Labour MP, desperate to lure voters back to her party, repeated its line on Green policies.

"The environment should not be a priority over people - Labour puts people before the environment!"

"People are part of the environment," responded the Green. "Read your Polanyi!" he taunted.[25]

Karl Polanyi's work *The Great Transformation* was widely read during the 2020s. The works of Hayek and Friedman[26] on the 'right' and of Marx and Engels[27] on the 'left' were superseded by an emergent orthodoxy based on sustainable development. Polanyi's works resonated precisely because they rejected both 'right' and 'left' in favour of a nuanced and balanced approach to radical reform. The taunt 'read your Polanyi' had a colloquial meaning among parliamentarians which - roughly translated – meant 'don't be such an ignoramus'. The Labour MP, stung by the rebuke, went silent – she had not read her Polanyi.

Peter Dimbleby intervened to give Sharon one further opportunity to respond.

"We took big risks with *Apprentices*," she began. "We took the view that the catch phrase 'You're Fired' was symbolic of the worst management practice possible. We also questioned the wisdom of talent shows that eliminate people one-by-one. Why promote a 'winner takes all' culture?"

"A woman after my heart," whispered the Socialist to the Green.

"My party leader would kill for her popularity ratings," whispered the Green in response.

The Lib-Dem MP tried to contribute but was roundly ignored by everyone. This response was typical. Since the disastrous coalition with Tories (before the revolution) nobody had taken an interest in what they had to say.

All the panellists recognised that *Apprentices* broke new ground by not eliminating ('sacking') contestants one by one. Rather than the old system of celebrities passing judgement, applicants to the show had to enrol on a post-graduate course of study. Sharon created documentaries charting their highs and lows, reviving the spirit of *Vet's School*[28] and combining it with the ethical challenge of *The Secret Millionaire*.[29] Audiences warmed as they watched people struggle to reshape their lives and thinking: it proved a winning formula, particularly when the public chose who would progress to the live TV shows. The graduation ceremony was televised: those with the highest levels of public support received the academic prize of an invitation to appear on live shows. Warren, the applicant that Sharon rescued from prison, graduated with good support from the public.

"We want to explore new business practices," continued Sharon. "The phrase 'You're Fired' is now a bad joke. We want the kind of entrepreneurship that John Spedan Lewis envisaged.[30] Every contestant stays as long as they want to. The tension rises as we see who will get to the finishing line first."

"And each contestant has a mentor, I understand," clarified Peter Dimbleby, giving away that he had not yet watched the show.

"Yes," replied Sharon. "And they have one third of the vote. Contestants have another third and the public has the final third. At the beginning of each show, we reveal the previous week's results and update league tables. The cream that rises to the top is a direct result of the confidence they build in their mentors, fellow contestants and the general public. No celebrities determine the outcome of this show."

Sharon fixed her eyes firmly on Harold and directly answered his question.

"Harold's suggestion that this programme constitutes 'brainwashing' is ludicrous."

Peter Dimbleby acted out his role as chair.

"Any further response, Harold?"

Harold spat out his retort in a pretence of victory.

"She says it directly. She's putting the dangerous communist principles of John Spedan Lewis before the tried and tested entrepreneurial principles of Alan Sugar. That's brainwashing. She admits it."

"Tried and tested formula for fucking up people and society, you mean," interjected the Socialist MP, who loved to put BBC editorial guidelines to the test.

"So Alan Sugar was 'brainwashing' people in the past?" interjected the Labour MP, recovering her confidence.

"You're twisting Harold's words," replied the Tory.

"You can't have it both ways," asserted Peter Dimbleby. "If *Apprentices* brainwashes people," he said with due emphasis, "surely *The Apprentice* did too?"

"No way," protested the Tory MP. "You can't compare the natural laws of the free market with the communism of John Spedan Lewis."

"I'm not sure John Spedan Lewis would have considered himself a communist," interjected the New Co-operative representative.

"Natural Laws?" shouted the Labour MP before anyone could respond. "The free market wasn't based on science. It was designed by a tiny group of rich people, then imposed on the rest of us. There's nothing 'natural' about it."

For a few seconds, the spectacle resembled the political mud-slinging that took place during Prime Minister's Question Time at the turn of the 21st century.

Sharon sought Peter Dimbleby's permission to intervene again but the New Co-operative MP, who had held back up to this point, asserted her right to speak.

"*The Apprentice* showed the values of its age," she began. "The individual entrepreneur was lauded and praised. The media then, unlike now, didn't engage in any serious debate about different kinds of entrepreneurship. We've supported this show because it explores with great care the teachings of co-operative educators and social entrepreneurs. The public now have a proper chance to indicate which kind of entrepreneur they want to see running key industries. We're leaving behind a system based on the arbitrary appointment and sacking of people to satisfy the egos of business owners and party politicians. Could there be a more stupid approach to developing a modern economy? So, we support a TV show that explores how individual, collective and public wisdom can play a productive role in shaping the co-operative entrepreneurship we want to see. That's what this programme captures. *Apprentices* is a symbol of *this* age, not Alan Sugar's."

"I wish my party leader could make speeches like that," said the Labour MP to the Green.

"Let's open this out to the audience," suggested Peter Dimbleby. "Yes, sir, in the third row?"

"What a load of hogwash," said the audience member. "There has to be a boss…"

"Have you been watching the show, sir?" asked Peter.

"Bits of it," he replied, hesitantly.

"Then you will appreciate that contestants are free to choose or reject a boss for each task."

"I wouldn't let that happen in my company," he replied.

Laughter broke out, and Sharon took advantage of the burst of laughter to get in another point.

"Alan Sugar never gave his teams a choice – he made them choose a leader even when there was only two in the team!" she said, with a tone verging on contempt. "We don't insist that contestants choose a leader. We've just seen a team without a nominated leader beat a team that had one. Maybe it depends on the task? Maybe it depends on the people? The format encourages us to rethink the nature of leadership. When is a leader needed? When does a leader make things worse?"

"As I say, left-wing nonsense," the company owning audience member reiterated lamely.

"Real life!" retorted the Green MP. "If you go camping with your friends, do you choose a leader?"

"No – but it's different at work!" was the reply.

"Why? Camping is unpredictable and complex. Workplaces are ritualised and routine. Why d'you need a leader for simple routine tasks when you don't need one for unpredictable and complex situations?"

"We've time for one last comment," interjected Peter.

A young woman stood up and took the microphone.

"Would the panel comment on press rumours that the producer of *Apprentices* was seen kissing one of the contestants?"

The room hushed. Sharon froze. She wondered if Warren was watching.

"Well," responded Peter. "That's all we have time for this week. Next week we'll be broadcasting from Edinburgh, Scotland where the panellists will include the Scottish President and newly elected Prime Minster. If you want to be part of the audience to debate the first five years of Scottish Independence[31], you can send an email to qh@bbc.coop – it's on the screen now. We look forward to seeing you there. From all of us here, good night!"

VII

Warren reaches the final of *Apprentices*...

The lights were low. Warren and Polyana stood in the wings of the TV stage looking at two empty executive chairs at opposite sides of a circular table. On either side of them were a pair of Board members, seated and ready to ask them questions. Warren heard Cliff's voice in his earpiece.

"And just to confirm what you are calling your pitch?" asked Cliff, pointing to a document given to him by Warren.

"The *FairShares Model*" Warren responded warmly.[32]

Warren recognised three of the Dragons from his previous appearance on this stage - Cliff, Adriana and Davina. Back then, it had ended badly when he was marched away by Officer Natasha. The fourth Board member was Harold Porter, the outspoken advocate of capitalism who had confronted Peter Dimbleby on *Question Hour* six weeks early. Sharon realised that he was an audience draw now that he was tipped to be the next leader of the New Conservative Party.

Warren's apprehension had a different quality this time. It stemmed not from his ignorance of the subject at hand, but from a fear that he now knew too much. Would it be possible to communicate his idea in a short space of time? As a graduate of the BBC's course on social and sustainable enterprise management, Warren knew he was quite popular with the public. And with each passing week his share of the public vote had increased slightly. However, he found it much harder to win the support of mentors and contestants. Overall, he had climbed to second place on the *Apprentices* leader board.

For the grand finale, the top two contestants headed teams trying to win one million MPMs provided by the BBC, plus additional capital that the BBC would raise through a crowd investing programme. The winning team would use this capital to develop their social enterprise. Warren was up against Polyana Abramovich, daughter of a jailed Russian tycoon, who had appeared before him on the *Dragons' Cave* two years ago.

Polyana had been popular after the screening of the documentaries but her support had waned with the public during the live shows. However, she was well liked by mentors and fellow contestants because of her encyclopaedic knowledge of banking. After nine weeks, Polyana was still the front runner:

Cumulative Voting – Week 9

	Mentors	*Contestants*	*Public*	*Total*
Polyana	35%	38%	10%	27.7%
Warren	18%	17%	38%	24.3%
Andy	19%	10%	18%	15.7%
Yasmin	12%	14%	8%	11.3%
Jane	7%	7%	3%	5.7%
Osman	4%	3%	9%	5.3%
Ben	2%	10%	2%	4.7%
Philip	2%	0%	6%	2.7%
Simon	1%	1%	4%	2.0%
Tim	0%	0%	2%	0.7%
	100%	100%	100%	

A further 12 contestants had dropped out. The experience of getting less than 0.5% of the public vote was hard to bear. And while contestants were spared the sack by a celebrity entrepreneur, some chose to fire themselves to save their egos from further damage.

For the finale, the scores were wiped clean. All constituencies were briefed to support the best idea, not their favourite contestant. Inevitably, the press turned it into a popularity contest between Polyana and Warren with copious profiles of each in the run up to the final.

Cliff also spoke to Polyana via her earpiece.

"And just to confirm, what are you calling your idea?" he asked, pointing out the other document before him.

"The *Working People's Bank*", she replied.[33]

The lights came up. The music started. While Polyana and Warren remained in the shadows, Ed emerged from the wings and moved to the centre of the stage. He was relishing his chance to act as Master of Ceremonies.

VIII

Warren waits (again) in the wings…

"Nervous?" asked Sharon, placing her hand on Warren's forearm.

"Yes," smiled Warren, placing his hand on top of hers.

Sharon's interest in Warren had continued to grow, much more so than the other contestants. Once the media had reported their backstage kiss there was no point keeping their relationship a secret. As for the other contestants, even after extensive re-education, their arrogance remained. It was rare for them to express any remorse for their anti-social investing. On the contrary, their assumptions of innate superiority seemed to grow stronger as they became convinced the BBC was grooming them for future greatness.

Warren continued to be different. He would not join in backstage chat about the contestants' superior 'breeding'. Warren took a different view, that it was purely a matter of chance that this group of investors had lucked their way into Sharon's programme. Breeding had nothing to do with their collective good fortune. They were unremarkable, just like reality TV stars everywhere.

"You'll be fine," said Sharon. With Ed going through the opening routine showing videos of each team's activities to the studio audience, Sharon and Warren enjoyed a few minutes together before the finale unfolded.

Warren clearly remembered the first time he met Sharon face-to-face, standing in this same spot just before his humiliation on the set of the *Dragons' Cave*.

"Have you run this show for long?" he asked.

"Almost two years now," Sharon replied, spotting immediately that Warren was reciting their former encounter.

"Is it fun?"

Sharon smiled.

"Yes. It's been fun," she replied. "All the more for you being here."

"Oh!" he responded, smiling.

"Can't imagine this being fun for the contestants?" he commented.

"I think we've made a lot of improvements," Sharon asserted. "No pompous Dragons' on this show. Are you tempted to pull out?" Sharon probed, hesitantly.

Warren studied Sharon closely. There had never been a woman he found more attractive, and not just because she kept herself trim with early morning runs. Her dress sense had evolved with their relationship. She wore a wider range of colours, but maintained the casual smartness that had caught his eye when they first met. He was pleased that she did not have children and was not married, and that her tasteful ethnic jewellery still adorned her wrists and neck. She still wore stylish leather boots with matching leather trousers - a tribute to the way their lives were now rocking. Warren still liked the way her blouse hugged the curves of her upper body. He no longer wondered if the woman inside was as agreeable as the outfit - he knew it to be the case.

"I wouldn't let you down like that, Sharon."

"You'll be fine," I promise. "I've not seen any of the Apprentices eaten by the Board yet," she reassured.

"Not physically," commented Warren. "But I have seen some get a good battering."

"It happens, but mainly to people who under-estimate the other Board members," she replied with a smile.

"Any words of wisdom?" asked Warren, amazed at the way their initial conversation was coming back to him almost word for word.

"Roll with the punches," she said with the confidence of a trainer guiding their prize fighter before a hostile encounter.

"I will," he said with a smile.

As if Fate was watching over them both, Sharon's phone rang at precisely that moment.

"Yes," she said in a neutral tone. Then Sharon beamed with pleasure. "Hi!" she replied. "Where are you at the moment?"

Sharon nodded.

"Good. I'll see you in the party room after the final. And keep your mother under control."

"Anything interesting?" asked Warren.

"That's your date for after the show," replied Sharon.

"*You're* my date after this show," he replied.

"Well, this time you'll have to share me. There's someone keen to meet you. A big fan of yours," Sharon replied mischievously.

"I can hardly wait," answered Warren, sarcastically.

Sharon and Warren watched as Ed rounded off the first section of the show, then heard the 30 second warning in their earpieces.

Sharon led Warren to the edge of the stage.

"See you soon," she said.

"Wish me luck?" he asked.

Sharon showed him that the fingers of her right hand were crossed, then pushed him firmly towards the stage with her left hand. Warren walked onto a cross that marked the place where the spotlight would introduce him to the studio audience.

"No battering tonight," said Warren to himself, preparing to stride out confidently.

IX

Opening statements...

"Contestants," announced Ed, "we have watched you working with your teams to prepare for this moment. We have been scrutinising your plans. Now is your chance to close the deal ..."

As a familiar snippet of music played, Ed glanced at the Board to check they were in place. He saw Davina helping Adriana adjust her seat. Across the table he saw that Cliff and Harold were ready.

Ed, the MC, felt at ease.

"You will both have one minute to introduce your ideas," he announced. "Then the Board will cross-examine each of you for five minutes. Next, you will have three minutes to question each other face-to-face. Lastly, you'll have one minute for your closing statements. Then the voting will begin!"

Harold was enjoying this twist of events. His ceaseless campaign against *Apprentices* had prompted an invitation from Sharon to participate in the final. It was Sharon's preferred strategy for containing him as she thought he would find it harder to attack the show if he was to appear on it. Harold wanted opportunities to appear on prime time TV to raise his political profile. His ego got the better of his intellect and he accepted Sharon's offer.

After a second jingle the spotlights glowed brightly, revealing Polyana and Warren to the audience.

"Contestants!" Ed announced loudly. "Please take your seats between the Board members."

Polyana and Warren advanced in tandem and rotated the executive chairs prepared for them. On the table were cups of water, pens, paper and neatly laid out communication plans. As this week's contestant representatives on the Board, it was their job to pitch on behalf of their teams. It was the job of the other Board members to ask intelligent questions and make sure that everyone with a vote made the most informed and intelligent choice.

Cliff looked directly at Polyana.

"Your opening statement please."

"My idea is the *Working People's Bank.* Over the last 20 years, our banking system has been through a series of reforms. Customers can now elect some directors. Workforces can elect auditors to provide them with reports on their bank managers' performance. Banks now pay the Treasury fees for any digital money they create.

"All these things have helped. But it is not enough. Ownership by absentee investors is the legacy of the Dark Age. It is time to have banks that fund managers cannot control in which only basic rate taxpayers can hold shares. Anyone paying a higher rate of tax can deposit money, use bank services and earn interest on their savings, but the profits will be distributed amongst basic rate taxpayers. The *Working People's Bank* will finally give people back the wealth that was stolen from them a generation ago. I look forward to your questions."

Polyana paused and there was a ripple of applause from the live audience.

Warren smiled at the other members of the Board. Cliff invited him to give his opening statement and the clock started ticking.

"My idea is the *FairShares Model,*" began Warren. "This encourages multi-stakeholder, member-owned enterprises that spread wealth, knowledge and power fairly. Multi-stakeholder enterprises are not new. Member-owned enterprises are not new. But many of them lack the mechanisms needed to tackle inequalities that remain entrenched in our society. Why? Because they share only trading profits, not the full value of an enterprise's assets.

We still allow the ideas of our intellectuals to be stolen from them. We still steal the products of labour from the labourer. We still allow the privatisation of knowledge.

"The *FairShares Model* counters all this. It shares out all the benefits of ownership, not just a cash surplus from trading. It shares power and knowledge amongst all its members, not just an executive elite. It promotes an open intellectual commons, not concealed vaults of private property. I look forward to your questions."

When he heard a ripple of applause, Warren was tempted to stand up and acknowledge the audience. Instead he smiled warmly in the hope that his face was being beamed into the homes of millions of TV viewers.

X

Cross-examination…

Ed turned to the first Board member.

"Davina, you have been randomly selected to start questioning Polyana. There are now five minutes to find out more about her idea starting….now!"

"Polyana," asked Davina kindly. "What's new about your idea?"

Polyana breathed a sigh of relief – of all the questions that could have been asked, this one was a gift.

"It introduces into our banking system a new dynamic. It starts to shift wealth back to the people who create it."

Harold could be audibly heard scoffing at the idea that 'basic rate taxpayers' were wealth creators. Polyana immediately responded.

"Harold!" she said accusingly. "Have you researched this issue? Ellerman's work[34] is absolutely clear on who adds value during production, and Patterson[35] established that workforces risk a similar amount to investors when they commit their labour to an enterprise. Working people still can't move their labour as easily as investors can move their capital. The Share Dealing and Securities Act helps but it doesn't go far enough. We need to use ownership to accelerate the wealth shift."

"But co-operative banks aren't new," interjected Cliff, "we've had them operating successfully around the globe for over a hundred years, and all forms of mutual finance have enjoyed a steadily increasing share of the market over the last 20 years."[36]

Polyana had expected this.

"But co-operative banks and credit unions – while they are set up to help people on lower incomes - are open to everyone. The more successful they are, the more middle class people move their money into them and the more interest is paid to the middle classes. Don't we need a better way to get capital into the hands of the poorest 50% of the population? I think we need a better strategy to increase their share of national wealth."

Cliff nodded. Polyana was sharp and it was easy to see why she had the support of many mentors and contestants. Cliff felt a dash of guilt. He was one of the middle classes she was talking about. After he retired, he moved all his money out of private banks into an internet credit union called Zopa. He'd done well out of it.[37]

"So why is your idea different?" repeated Davina, who still felt that she had not received an answer.

"Because the ownership criteria are different," she replied. "Think of how the Grameen Bank[38] started in Bangladesh. It was a member-owned bank where the qualification was owning less than half an acre of land. Within a generation, six million people had become bank owners with access to credit. They built local enterprises. They set aside money for welfare. They even helped the country out when hit by floods."

Polyana paused a moment to see whether this was registering with the Board members. She was confident of their attention and decided to drive home her point.

"So how do you apply that *here*?" she continued. "You clearly can't use a half-acre of land. That would include far too many people – including all those yuppies like me living in shoebox apartments in expensive parts of London. No. In our culture, the basic rate taxpayer is a clear criterion. It identifies the section of the population we most want to help."

"But won't people hide their income status from the bank," stated Harold. "How will you stop fraud?"

"Require the production of payslips or tax returns each year. The bank has many checks to do, so why not this one?" she replied.

"Just as I thought," replied Harold. "The bureaucracy will be a nightmare!"

"Hardly onerous," she retorted. "Surely you remember what it was like when our government was fighting that illegal 'war on terror'?"

The audience rumbled. Cliff chuckled as he recalled the jailing of Tony Blair. Polyana continued to make her point.

"To open an account I needed two bills, a passport or driving licence and had to give a whole host of irrelevant details so that bank workers could check I was who I said I was. Hell, sometimes I couldn't make changes to my own account over the phone because I couldn't remember some trivial little detail about my past!"

"Okay," responded Harold. "What will you do with all us 'rich' people? Are you going to cut off our banking?"

"Not at all, not at all," Polyana responded confidently. "The state hasn't taken over all the private banks. You still have some choice. At the *Working Peoples' Bank,* you'll be able to open an account, get all the normal banking services, save your money and earn good interest. We'll guarantee a return on your savings linked to the growth in the economy. The only difference is that you can't own shares. Only basic rate tax payers will be able to own the shares."

"But you can't have working people bearing all that risk!" exclaimed Harold.

"We bore it in 2008," replied Polyana. "Did you argue for higher taxes on the rich after the crash? No, you made the poor pay by cutting public services *and* depressing wages. *We* paid the bill. *We* took the risk. *Not* you."

Polyana sounded convincing even though she was not a basic rate taxpayer herself. She did a good job of speaking as if she was one and this resonated well with both Board members and the public.

"And how will they buy shares?" interjected Adriana.

"We'll do co-operative share offers," replied Polyana.

"But co-operative shares don't increase in value," replied Adriana. "So how will working people increase their wealth?"

"Well that's something we should rethink," said Polyana. "Not everything about the old private sector was bad. Having a good way to represent the *future* value of an organisation is one of them."

Warren, who had been listening intently, suddenly came to life and started writing notes. He would get his chance to quiz Polyana later.

"I fully understand why co-operative shares were designed the way they were originally," she continued. "It was a good way to limit returns to capital and ensure that more money was reinvested in job creation. But the issue was never the value of the shares. The issue was who held them and how they could be traded. If you control who can hold them, and limit the opportunities to trade them, it makes sense to represent the value of the enterprise in a share price."

"But if you limit their tradability, you'll also limit their value," interjected Adriana.

"In this case, you're still talking about 80% of the population. That's a lot of people. We want that 80% to be enriched in a sustainable way, ensuring others do not lose out. Pegging interest rates on savings to the growth rate of the economy ensures a win-win for everyone."

Whilst the Board were looking for holes in Polyana's argument Warren found himself nodding in agreement.

Polyana was coming to the end of her 5 minutes so she took the chance to make one last point.

"I've been reading Piketty's fabulous work.[39] He makes a simple but profound point. If the return on capital is higher than the growth of the economy, wealth is transferred to the owners of capital faster than to those who can only sell their labour. This will be true if working people don't own much capital. But if they do, *everything changes*. With my team's idea you can address this. By opening a bank where shares are allocated to basic rate taxpayers on the basis of their banking *activities*, the wealth created by banking will be channelled to them gradually. And it does so without the need for draconian taxes on the rich."

Warren felt admiration for his rival. It was a solid argument and complimented his own. It might be difficult to challenge her later.

As she made her final point, a familiar jingle marked the end of the first cross-examination. Polyana felt pleased. She'd been able to get her points across without Harold derailing her train of thought.

Ed walked to the front of the stage and the music died down. "Harold, you have been randomly selected to start the next cross-examination. Warren, your five minutes starts....now!"

Harold stared as if his gaze was a dagger in Warren's face. Harold had been the butt of Warren's acerbic wit since *Question Hour*. This was his chance for revenge.

"You say there is **theft** from our intellectuals and our labourers. Tell me - how does this theft occur because I've never seen it?"

"It's very simple," replied Warren. "Every time an employee creates something, the ownership of what they create is transferred to their employer. The legal person that is their employer gets ownership of everything the employee creates."

"But that can't be considered theft?" challenged Harold. "In these new co-operatives of yours, the workers are also co-owners of the property they create. They are producers and owners at the same time. They can't steal from themselves surely?"

Warren smiled. For all the changes he had been through, and notwithstanding all the commitments of the social economy that he now admired, he could not shake off the belief that there was still something in the liberalism of the eighteenth century worth defending.

"What can a person do with the works they have contributed to a social enterprise after they leave?" asked Warren rhetorically. "That's surely the best test of whether a person is enjoying the fruits of their labour?"

"And your point is?" asked Cliff who felt that Warren wasn't getting his point across.

"My point is that on leaving a co-operative, or social enterprise, few people feel a sense of ownership over what they have contributed, and few assume they can take contributions they have made and develop them at a new place of work. With all the changes we've had – many of which I admire – the alienation described by Marx is still with us today. It strikes me that any employer – whether private, state or social – still expects to have ownership of everything that is produced. Until every person owns what they produce – without question – alienation will always be possible."

"But surely it is never an individual effort?" interjected Davina.

"Of course, but go into any workplace and there's many small groups – and diligent people - who pull the ideas together to make them intelligible. It is these people - these groups in each enterprise - who deserve formal recognition for their efforts. It is these groups who can quickly lose the right to use the intellectual ideas they have created just by changing job."

"So, there's a bit of liberal in you after all," added Harold, subversively hoping his words would damage Warren's credibility with the public.

Warren paused. How should he answer this charge?

"Yes," he said tentatively. "Yes – there is a bit of a liberal in me, but for all working people not just a few 'entrepreneurs'. I can't shake off the idea that the group does better when it acknowledges and rewards the contributions of its members. I can't shake off the idea that when people pull together lots of good ideas and succeed in putting them into practice they should have an *inalienable right* to use them again whenever they wish and wherever they are. The question is *how* to ensure this happens."

Warren had not mentioned the *FairShares Model* so he quickly added....

"...and this is why the *FairShares Model* is so important. It commits the members of an organisation to recognising the efforts of other members. It is a workable system for overcoming the alienation identified by Marx."

This appeal to Marx annoyed Harold, as Warren knew it would. Warren knew that Harold would never read Marx sufficiently well to appreciate the ambiguity of his commitments to liberalism and communism. But equally he knew that Adriana would welcome this nuance. She had studied Warren's ideas and liked them, but she felt that he had not communicated the mechanism by which it would be achieved.

"And you are proposing that all documents produced at work are automatically licenced using Creative Commons? Is that right?"[40]

"Yes, yes," said Warren hastily. "And the *FairShares Model* is an excellent mechanism for advancing Creative Commons at work," he added quickly.

In his mind, Warren felt that his ideas were clear but he was never sure if he was communicating them to people watching. He kept searching for simple ways to convey them.

"So that's the first idea. The creation of an *intellectual commons* in the workplace. The *FairShares Model* starts with a contractual agreement amongst the members of an enterprise that all works belong to their creators. Then, the creators of ideas reciprocate by granting everyone else a licence to use their works. People at work will *own* the fruits of their labour, but everyone else will have a public or group right to *use* the fruits of their labour."

"And the second idea?" prompted Adriana, sidelining Harold's attempt to interrupt the questioning.

"My second big idea is *value-added sharing*."

"How's that different from profit-sharing?"

"Basically, it's a process for allocating entitlements to the value of an enterprise's current and future assets. Profits each year are only a tiny part of the value of an enterprise – the rest is often hidden or unrealised."

Warren paused to take a sip of water. What he said now would be important to his team's chance of winning.

"Take a medical social enterprise that gets approval for a new drug. If this drug is safe, inexpensive and easy to produce, it transforms the value of the enterprise overnight. But it doesn't change its cash or profit position overnight."

All the Board members were nodding, but Warren still felt that he had not communicated his idea in a way that people at home would grasp.

"It is fairer to allocate shares of wealth when they are created than to do so retrospectively - perhaps years later - when cash and profits are generated. The one thing I did like about the share system of the private economy was its *future* orientation: it was a mechanism for rewarding today's efforts in a way that bore fruit in the future. I accept we didn't do this in a fair and transparent way, and that shares were allocated for the wrong contributions, but the system itself had some merit."

"Where did you find the *FairShares Model*?" asked Cliff.

"I found several papers about it in a research archive. There was an association - the FairShares Association[41] – which lasted for a few years. It stopped publishing after 2018. Up until then, it published many innovative ideas. For example, its members advocated issuing shares for human, intellectual and social capital investments, not just financial investments. They proposed that only 30% of a company's dividends should go to those making financial contributions. The rest would go to those making entrepreneurial, labour and trading contributions. My team are convinced that this enterprise design enfranchises everyone who makes an important contribution to an enterprise. In short, it is fairer, so we call it the *FairShares Model.*"

And with that, the jingle sounded again. It marked the end of Warren's first cross-examination. He felt perplexed about his performance and was relieved it was over. But he had little time to relax. No sooner had he taken a sip of water, Ed announced that Polyana would now proceed to quiz him some more.

XI

The face-to-face debate…

"Sound awfully complicated," queried Polyana.

Warren said nothing and soon the silence became awkward. He suddenly realised that Polyana was not just making a statement. She was expecting him to respond.

"The mechanism is complex, but the idea is simple," he eventually replied. "My team have published all the technical details on the *Apprentices* website. There are model rules for associations, co-operatives and companies. There are system designs to make each process work. The concept is simple: **each person's share in the future wealth of their community can be defined by the contributions they make to the organisations they use, work for and buy from.** Contributions are made in many ways: generating ideas of value; voluntary labour; paid work; extraordinary investments of time, effort and energy in specific projects; raising a family; caring for friends and relatives; and, of course, how people spend their income and invest their savings. All these can be crafted into 'qualifying contributions' for shares in different types of social enterprise."[42]

"Is it *too* complicated?" asked Polyana.

Warren started to understand her strategy. She hoped to win the one million MPMs by insinuating that Warren's idea was impractical. So, with a flash of inspiration, Warren linked his idea to Polyana's.

"The *FairShares Model* would be ideal for your bank. It would make your bank work," he asserted.

Polyana was unsure how to react.

"Really, er…ask me about that in a moment," she replied. Warren noticed her hesitation and used it to his advantage.

"Your project has a clear need to entrench a 'qualifying contribution' for shares. The notion of a 'qualifying contribution' is at the heart of the *FairShares Model.* It looks like it's at the heart of the *Working People's Bank* too."

Warren felt relief as he finally found a way to show his idea was simple in practice.

"When you establish a *FairShares* enterprise, you have to decide what the qualifying contributions are for issuing shares to workers and customers. You described yours really well – that owners must be basic rate tax payers. So the *FairShares Model* is perfect for your project. You can adopt a *FairShares Model* constitution, establish the qualifying contribution for shares as being a staff member or account holder who pays the basic rate of tax, and issue shares when this criterion is satisfied."

Polyana wanted to interrupt Warren's flow, but she struggled to think of a way to do it. Luckily, Warren was satisfied that he had made the point he needed to make and did not want to dilute the effect by carrying on unnecessarily. Polyana, on the other hand, did not want to give Warren a further opportunity to use her idea to build the case for *FairShares*. Both stopped speaking and Ed had to intervene to get them going again.

"Warren, why don't you ask Polyana a question?"

To Polyana's annoyance, Warren decided to pick up the questioning where she had left it.

"So, Polyana, you have clear criterion for becoming an owner?"

"Yes," responded Polyana.

"And what will happen when a person's income puts them into a higher tax bracket?"

"My team believe their financial holding should be converted to a loan account that attracts fixed interest. That way, the return on their capital is tied to the growth rate of the economy."

"So it becomes a debt rather than an asset. Have you considered the effects of that on the solvency of the bank?" quizzed Warren.

Polyana had not, so she remained quiet. Warren pressed on with another question.

"If a person has earned a share of future wealth based on their past contributions, is it not an injustice to remove it from them?"

"We're not removing it," responded Polyana. "We're fixing its value."

"What about incentives?" queried Warren

Polyana was not sure where he was going with his argument.

"A guarantee of interest is fair."

"Well, it just strikes me that a person consistently earning *less* than the tax threshold could get a *greater* share of future wealth than someone who reaches it. It's like the early 21st century poverty trap in which doing more work lost you benefits.[43] If I'm close to a threshold, I won't want to breach it. I'll want my shares to keep accumulating. But if I reach the threshold, you'll cancel my shares and fix the value. Isn't that a disincentive to progress at work?"

Polyana thought that Warren had made a mistake. It gave her a chance to take a moral stand about wealth inequality and make it look as if Warren was defending the rich.

"But what about all that Stanford and Harvard research we studied together on wealth inequalities?[44] Don't you recall that the poorest 50% of the population in the US held only 0.5% of stocks and shares?

"Yes, I remember," said Warren.

"And do you remember that the top 1% owned over 50%," continued Polyana preparing to inject a little poison into Warren credibility.

"You are in that 1%, I presume?" she said accusingly.

"Yes, I probably am," said Warren. "And so are you," he retorted.

"Touché," thought Polyana. Warren was quick in his counter attack. As she hesitated slightly, Warren threw in a new question.

"Is your idea sufficiently creative, Polyana? It looks to me like a rehash of Mondragon's 'Bank of the People's Labour'"

"Yes," she replied unashamedly. "It draws inspiration from that and also from the Grameen Bank. But my team's concept is to find the best application in an advanced economy. My team thought Mondragon's approach still acted more for the middle class than the working class."

Warren was about to disagree but he was stopped by a jingle that marked the end of the face-to-face debate. He wanted to continue challenging Polyana by suggesting the bank's success would also be its demise by systematically turning assets into liabilities.

He had run out of time and had to give way to Ed. Relishing his MC role once again, Ed moved to the front of the stage to introduce the final phases of the show.

XII

Closing statements…

“Contestants,” he said. “Please prepare your final remarks.”

A specially prepared piece of music that lasted 60 seconds gave each contestant the opportunity to jot down their ideas. Cameras above the table zoomed in to give the audience a few clues on what each of them was planning to say.

Warren wrote ‘be generous, be fair and sell fairness.’

Polyana’s notes included ‘simplicity v complexity, practicality v impracticality’.

The music ended.

“Warren,” said Ed. “Your closing statement is first.”

Warren took a risk.

“Ladies and gentlemen,” he began. “I like Polyana’s idea. It makes sense to me. It is fair in principle and likely to be fair in practice.”

Polyana scrutinised Warren. What on earth was he doing defending her idea? Why was he not attacking it?

“I want to be sure Polyana’s idea will work,” he continued. “How can we secure ownership and control rights for basic taxpayers? At the same time, how can we be sure that basic rate taxpayers won’t abuse their power? How can we be sure they won’t take advantage of higher-rate taxpayers once they have control? The answer is a multi-stakeholder constitution.”

“That’s why the *FairShares Model* is the missing ingredient. It ensures a balance of powers that can be locked into Polyana’s bank. My team have looked at her idea – and we all like it. But Polyana is not proposing a fair constitution to implement her idea for fairness. To secure her team’s vision and to keep it fair, a *FairShares* constitution is needed.

In its absence, as nearly always happens, one group will systematically improve its own position at the expense of others."

The Board members and contestants were somewhat surprised at Warren's remarks. It sounded like he wanted Polyana's idea to succeed as much as his own.

"Polyana," said Ed. "Your closing remarks please."

"Ladies and Gentlemen," she opened. "My idea is simple, straightforward, practical and doable. Warren's idea is complex, esoteric, impractical and unrealisable. The way my enterprise idea will transfer wealth to working people is clear. The way Warren's idea transfers wealth is unclear. The way our constitution will work is clear. Warren's constitutional ideas are nebulous and tortuous to put into practice. You have a clear choice before you. Please back my idea then join our bank."

Polyana had time to spare but said nothing more. She felt the choice was clear and did not want to muddy her message. In 30 short seconds, however, she distinguished herself from Warren. She was precision and clarity. Warren was ambiguity and difficulty.

But Warren also felt pleased. He sought to appeal to something positive in his audience - their desire to recognise and reward creativity and generosity. He felt Polyana over-simplified the choice by ignoring the inter-dependencies between people. Warren appealed to positive emotions and intelligence. Polyana appealed to basic emotions and logic.

XIII

Results…

The contestants withdrew from the round table and joined their teams. Ed interviewed some mentors who had been studying the materials uploaded to the *Apprentices* website. By discussing them on air, members of the public acquired a sense of what they contained and the attitudes of the mentors towards them.

After a commercial break, the 15 minute voting period began. Ed now turned to the Board. He chaired a session in which they deliberated and discussed the cross-examinations and face-to-face debate. It was their custom to be split in their views to entertain and inform the audience while mentors, contestants and the public cast their votes. Minutes ticked by and the votes rolled in: one million, two million, three million, four million. With a worldwide audience, the show attracted 23 million votes before the jingle sounded for the third commercial break.

When the show resumed, spotlights lit up Polyana and Warren who were walking from opposite sides of the stage to meet Ed who was standing centre stage.

"Polyana," started Ed. "So how do you rate your chances?"

"Better than even," she boasted. "My idea is simpler than Warren's and it is easier to implement. It benefits every person, not just working people. And I can see it happening in my lifetime," she closed.

"He had you on the run a bit during your face-to-face exchanges?" quizzed Ed.

Polyana fronted her response with all the confidence she could muster.

"It does not change the basic strength and simplicity of my team's idea."

"No it doesn't. No it doesn't. A round of applause for Polyana, ladies and gentlemen!"

Ed led the applause himself, then turned to Warren.

"Warren," he said deliberately and slowly, leaving the word hanging in the air whilst looking at the audience.

The applause died down and a few gigglers could be heard.

"Warren," Ed repeated. "A bit complicated?" he chimed, encouraging the gigglers to break into laughter.

Whilst in the wings, Warren had thought of a good response.

"It's like the *wePod 2030,* Ed," he replied. "It's a highly complex piece of engineering, and it's hard to understand how it works, but as soon as you use it you are overwhelmed by its elegance and beauty. I think that became clear during the debate."

"Indeed it did. Indeed it did," finished Ed. "A round of applause for Warren, ladies and gentlemen!"

As stage hands quickly reorganised the finalists for the announcement, video interviews with Polyana and Warren were shown to the public. They were full of media gunk, pressing the contestants to say 'how much it would mean' to win the show's prize. Then, finally, the moment to announce the winner was upon them.

Ed held up an envelope containing the name of the winner.

"Ladies and gentlemen," prompted Ed. "The winner is…."

Thump, thump, thump, the music moved in time to Polyana's and Warren's heart beats. As he waited, Warren's mind returned to his first encounter with the Dragons on this very stage. He'd been a bit foolish - he could see that now. But he was an honest fool. He had sincerely believed all his life that he had been doing his best. He looked back not so much with regret as with awe. He had grown up in the heart of a dishonest, corrupt, viciously competitive, destructively selfish business culture and still retained his humanity. If there was hope for him, there was hope for others.

The culture of collaboration created at the BBC, allowing students and educators, programme makers and contestants to freely develop their ideas had become a hot house of social innovation. It was in this culture that Warren's ideas were sculpted through numerous challenges and moulded by his team into something valuable. To Warren, the *FairShares Model* was imbued with aesthetic beauty as well as practical utility.

But what pleased him most was not the results of the creative endeavours he had pursued for 12 months. It was his sense that he had eradicated all trace of hostility toward 'others' (all those 'socialists', 'labourites', 'subversives', 'trade unionists', 'communists', 'social entrepreneurs', 'co-operators', 'greens' and 'radicals' his father had taught him to denigrate). They now had a wispy quality, like ghosts no longer to be feared, like distant childhood horrors that had finally been laid to rest. In the middle of the mayhem that was unfolding around him, he felt a warmth towards his fellow contestants that he had never felt before.

Thump, thump, thump…the beat continued.

"Polyana!" shouted Ed. And without understanding why, Warren found himself jumping for joy almost as much as his 'opponent'. He delighted in sharing the madness that was the first *Apprentices* finale. Glittering party poppers lit up by strobe lights created a mosaic of dancing shadows on everyone around him. In the mayhem, only a few people looked at the scoreboard. And Warren was one of them.

Final Vote – Week 10

	Mentors	*Contestants*	*Public*	*Total*
Polyana	75%	62%	15%	50.7%
Warren	25%	38%	85%	49.3%

Polyana had won by a whisker. Warren calmed right down as soon as he studied how the scores were made up. On contemplating the public vote, he felt his eyes moisten. He must have touched something in them, appealed to more than their desire for money and revenge. Perhaps he had touched their craving to give and receive praise, to be valuable and be part of things that were meaningful. Or perhaps it was just that the sight of a Bolshie former investment banker, saddled with an ASBO that prevented him from investing - and who had quietly and discreetly fallen in love with the producer of *Apprentices* - had wormed his way into the affections of the nation.

Warren could feel a tear rolling down his cheek. Sharon – misunderstanding his reaction - tried to comfort and console him. As soon as etiquette permitted, she led him away from the hubbub into the adjacent entertainment suite where they took a moment to hug each other.

As Board members and contestants left the stage to start a party, Warren saw Adriana and Cliff conversing with someone at a drinks counter. He also saw Officer Natasha who had arrested him nearly two years earlier. She was the woman who conspired with Sharon to get him to join *Apprentices*. Natasha smiled at him and raised her glass, then ominously started walking towards him.

XIV

The final denouement…

"So, was it worth it?" asked Natasha.

"Was it worth it!" he repeated, still thinking about the public vote.

"Did the punishment fit the crime?" she asked again.

"I don't feel punished," he replied, "I feel privileged. Not in the way I was privileged in the past, you realise. I mean I feel privileged to have found a sense of humility amongst so many fine people."

"Now, don't get carried away," replied Natasha. "Humble is not an adjective that I would ever use to describe you."

"Then I'll have to enjoy the feeling in the privacy of my own mind," he replied.

"You do that," said Natasha, taking his arm in a friendly way.

Warren noticed Natasha glance at Sharon who then nodded her consent as if saying 'yes, go on.'

"You're not arresting me again, are you?" said Warren, inquisitively. "Wherever I see you and Sharon together, I feel you are always planning something that's going to affect my future."

Natasha laughed.

"No, I'm not arresting you. But I do have someone I'd like you to meet."

Natasha led Warren in the direction of Adriana and Cliff.

"I know them already," said Warren.

"It's the person they are with," she replied.

As Warren approached, he recognised a third face but could not put a name to it.

"Warren," said Natasha. "I'd like to introduce you to my mother, Patricia."

"Have we met?" asked Warren.

"Not socially," replied Patricia. "I probably look different without my wig."

"Wig?" uttered Warren, as he suddenly realised that this was the judge who had rejected the appeal against his ASBO.

Warren turned inquiringly to Natasha.

"And you're definitely not arresting me, Natasha?" he asked again.

"No," definitely not. "My mother and I have been discussing an idea that involves you."

"Here we go again," said Warren. "In what way do you want my life to spiral out of control this time?"

"Well, I think it's time for a bit of normality, don't you?" replied Patricia.

"I don't understand," replied Warren.

"If I were to lift your ASBO, would you still commit your fortune to this *FairShares* idea?"[45]

Warren contemplated a new set of possibilities.

"I might want to go one better," he replied quickly.

"How so?" asked Cliff, whose interest was piqued.

"If you could get Polyana's team to consider a *FairShares* constitution, I might be tempted to move most of my fortune into her bank. The interest alone would be sufficient to fund *FairShares*. That bank is a project that will surely need a lot of supportive start-up capital."

"You wouldn't be buying a stake, you do realise that?" interrupted Adriana.

"No I would be depositing so much money in a savings account that the bank would have all the capital it needed to do some serious lending. I would expect a return that matched growth in the economy," confirmed Warren, showing how closely he'd been listening to Polyana during the show.

"It will probably be only a few per cent a year!" sparked Adriana.

It was Warren's turn to laugh.

"Yes, it will be," he said, remembering their first encounter. "And that's why a fair constitution will be necessary to give some voice to other stakeholders. I would be nervous – and I think all people like me would be nervous – if there was no mechanism to ensure that those modest interest payments were maintained.

"I'd like to ask for two things, Judge," Warren continued. "Firstly, I'd like to inject one million MPMs directly into the *FairShares* project. That's the same as the prize Polyana won in this competition. And secondly, Cliff, would it be possible for you to organise a community share offer with the support of the BBC so that the millions of viewers who supported me tonight can quickly become co-owners of a new *FairShares Investment Fund*?"

"Yes, I can do that," he replied. Cliff beckoned Sharon to ask for the BBC's help. As she walked over to join the conversation, Warren noticed that Natasha nodded to her again. They seemed to be acknowledging to each other that their efforts had been successful.

"And can I draw a modest salary while working on the project?" asked Warren. "Sufficient enough to be sure I can pay my bills while travelling around the world to promote the idea."

"I'll allow you to draw the funds you need to pay for that," replied Judge Patricia.

"Thank you," affirmed Warren. The Judge turned to Cliff and Adriana who had been taking an interest in this new development.

"Who would like to break the news to Polyana that she has a chance to close a deal that injects nearly three billion MPMs into her new bank?" asked the Judge.

"Perhaps we should ask her to match fund Warren's contribution?" queried Adriana.

"Strangely," said Judge Patricia, "I'm not entirely convinced that Polyana has earned the right to have her ASBO lifted yet, but I'll consider it shortly."

The Judge wanted to see how Polyana reacted to Warren's offer before considering her ASBO. She had not shown the same generosity of spirit towards Warren that he had shown towards her. Was Polyana still a competitive - rather than a collaborative - person? The Judge believed her rehabilitation might take a bit longer.

"Okay, I'll give her the news," said Adriana. She grabbed Cliff and slowly they started to look for Polyana.

"Cliff," prompted Patricia. "Will you be coming back?"

Cliff nodded and smiled.

"Good," said the Judge agreeably. "Now," she said turning to her daughter, Natasha. "Are you satisfied that this citizen has been fully rehabilitated?"

Natasha, still holding Warren's arm, nodded firmly.

"Beyond my wildest dreams. My *wildest* dreams," she confirmed.

"Okay," said the Judge. "I will ask the court to draw up the terms of this agreement. Citizen Buffet," she added sardonically, "you will need to meet with Natasha and myself later this week to sign off the terms. I'm agreeing to the immediate lifting of your ASBO."

"Thank you, Judge," smiled Warren who was starting to feel whole again.

"And remember, young man, you have many fans out there now. Make them proud."

"He will…" asserted Sharon, "…because if he doesn't there's no way I'll ask him to marry me."

"You'll ask me to what?" asked a startled Warren.

"Don't tease!" remonstrated Natasha. "There's only so much bad news a guy can take in a day."

Warren ignored the remark and fixed his eyes on Sharon. Sharon fixed her eyes on Warren.

Time passed.

"Excuse me?" chirped Natasha, wondering if she had become invisible.

Warren smiled. Sharon smiled.

"Cliiiiffff!" shouted Natasha, calling him back to the discussion.

"I think you'd better get these two a room!"

Appendix A – Key Moments in History

In the run up to this story…

1997	Financial Crisis (Asia)
2001	Financial Crisis (South America)
2005	Formation of Patient Opinion
2007	UN Principles of Responsible Management Education
2008	Financial Crisis (UK/US)
2012	Financial Crisis (Eurozone States)
2012	UN International Year of Cooperatives
2013	Leveson Report (December Revision)

In the future…

2015	Formation of Employee Opinion
2016	Formation of Citizen Opinion
2018	Financial Regulation Act (Repeal of the right to broker stocks and shares)
2018	ASBO Reform Act (Extension to Investors and Financial Speculators)
2018	Participatory Democracy Act
2019	Members Direct Declaration (Freedom of Association, Speech and Thought).
2019	First Police Reform Act (Citizen Courts and ASBOs)
2019	Share Dealing Amendment Act (Companies Act)
2020	Digital Money Act (Eurozone Regulations)
2020	Employment Relations Act (Repeal of Disciplinary and Grievance Rights for Employers).
2025	Share Dealing and Securities Act
2030	Social Democracy Act
2030	Second Police Reform Act (Rights of Suspects in Custody)

Appendix B – Working with Students

If you are using this book to stimulate discussion amongst students, here are some questions you can ask them.

Chapter I

- What are the differences between municipal enterprises, socialised enterprises, private enterprises and nationalised enterprises?
- What is a mediator, and why might one be more helpful to a co-operative than an HR consultant after a dispute at work?
- What is a member-owned business? How does it differ from an investor-owned business?

Chapters II and III

- What is the “rule of law”?
- Is the process of law making fair to all sections of society? (If yes, how is this fairness achieved? If not, how would you make it fairer?)
- Is social justice possible without sending people to jail? What alternatives would you consider?

Chapter IV

- What is a solidarity co-operative? How might it differ from other co-operatives and social businesses?
- What happened to the Co-operative Bank in 2013? Should it be able to keep ‘co-operative’ in its name?
- What is sustainable development? Do co-operatives / social enterprises make sustainable development more or less likely?

Chapter V

- What is free speech? What limitations – if any – should be placed on it?
- What is the difference between charity and social enterprise?

- What is civil society? What would disappear from a community if civil society could not develop?

Chapter VI, VII and VIII

- What is the effect of stock market trading at all hours of the day all around the world?
- Would the measures suggested in the novel (fixed trading days, criminalisation of stockbroking) stabilise the economy?
- Should ASBOs (anti-social behaviour orders) be extended to punish people who invest in projects that harm people and the environment?

Chapter IX

- How credible is Polyana's idea for a working people's bank in which only basic rate taxpayers can hold shares?
- What impact would Polyana's idea have if a 'people's bank' averaged £10 billion profits a year for 10 years with an average customer base of 5 million people?
- What are the 'benefits of ownership' that Warren refers to? What benefits are available to business owners that are not available to (most) employees?

Chapter X

- Who creates value in a business?
- What is a credit union? How does it differ from a conventional bank?
- Find out how co-operatives and private businesses calculate dividend payments. Which approach do you prefer and why?

Chapter XI

- Find out all you can about Creative Commons. Should a 'commons' approach or a 'private' approach to ownership of creative works be the preferred norm?

- What does Warren mean by a 'qualifying contribution' for shares? How do people qualify for shares in a *FairShares* Company?
- Find out all you can about the Caja Laborale (Bank of the People's Labour) in Mondragon. What is the role of the Caja Laborale in developing a social economy?

Chapter XII and XIII

- Would *you* vote for Polyana's or Warren's idea?
- Who do you see as 'radical' in your country?
- Was Nelson Mandela a radical?

Chapter XIV

- Should Judge Patricia lift Polyana's ASBO? (If yes, why? If not, why not?)
- Is a collaborative or competitive market economy the most likely to achieve sustainable development?
- Should Warren support Polyana's bank? (Why? / Why not?)

Postscript

If you enjoyed this story, the Creative Commons Licence under which it was published allows you to share it freely with friends and work colleagues providing you do not sell it, or the rights to it, without the consent of its creator.

The Postscript section will help you if you plan to use this story in a Higher Education setting. It provides information on the sources of the ideas that are discussed.

Dear Reader,

I've called this story 'a science faction novella'. This captures the way the story combines fact (when set in the present) and fiction (when set in the future). Whilst all the characters are fictional, some of the ideas discussed, and initiatives and organisations described, are not. I thought it may be interesting to provide comments so you can distinguish fact from fiction.

Best wishes

R J Ridley-Duff

The Dragons – the initial idea for the story came from conversations relating to a Dragons' Den that took place at 'Footsey', a social economy trade fair on 3rd March 2011 at Doncaster Racecourse in the UK. That year, I had an exhibitors' stand near the Dragons' Den and ended up in discussion with visitors about the way it reproduces the *status quo* rather than challenges it. The logic of social enterprise (at least during its formative years) was that labour hires capital. It follows from this that a social enterprise Dragons' Den should involve investors pitching their money to workers' leaders or social entrepreneurs, not – as was happening – social entrepreneurs pitching their business ideas to (social) investors. I felt they were reproducing the culture and norms of *private* enterprise, not creating a *social* enterprise alternative. Some of my MSc students then explored the issue by doing an exploratory dramatization of a Dragons' Den during a module called "Strategies for Change" (early 2012). After that, I put pen to paper and started writing.

Chapter Notes

[1] **Mediation** - there was active consideration given to compulsory mediation in employment disputes in 2007 when the UK government was working towards repealing statutory disciplinary and grievance regulations. In 2009, statutory procedures for D&G were repealed to restore voluntary agreements backed by a new code of conduct.

In the US, there was a large case in which courts required a mediation scheme at work. Courts insisted that the US Postal Service introduce compulsory mediation (if requested by an employee) to avoid a class action by ethnic minorities over equality issues. The employer, however, could not force an employee into mediation – it had to be requested or accepted by the employee. For more details see:

Ridley-Duff, R., & Bennett, A. (2011). "Towards mediation: developing a theoretical framework to understand alternative dispute resolution", *Industrial Relations Journal*, 42(2), 106-123.

2 **The BBC** is, of course, not a co-operative. However, it has some unambiguous co-operative / mutual characteristics such as 'licensees' (i.e. members) providing capital in return for public interest broadcasting. Unlike a co-operative, however, it is subject to statutory controls and the state can interfere (and take editorial control) during a 'national emergency' or 'terrorist incident'. It does not have a democratically elected board.

3 **Social enterprise** is a term that has been taken up all around the world. Through authoring *Understanding Social Enterprise: Theory and Practice* as well as supporting the work of *Social Enterprise Europe,* I've acquired knowledge of social enterprise education developing in the UK, Ireland, Austria, Germany, Greece, Switzerland, Poland, Indonesia, Japan, Montenegro, Ukraine and Croatia. My colleagues have worked across South East Asian (China, Malaysia, Korea and Philippines) and pioneered initiatives in Africa (Nigeria, Ghana, East Africa). It is by no means a UK/US concept.

Ridley-Duff, R. and Bull, M. (2011) *Understanding Social Enterprise: Theory and Practice,* London: Sage Publications.

4 **Solidarity Co-operatives** are multi-stakeholder enterprises that involve producers, consumers and supporters. In Italy there are now thousands of social co-operatives (many clustered in the Bologna region) that integrate the interests of public authorities, health professionals, marginalised workers and parents/carers. They are also a recognised legal form in Quebec, Canada, providing the legal form of choice for food production and social care co-operatives.

Co-operatives UK added a 'multi-stakeholder' classification in 2012 after working with Prof Johnston Birchall on a new classification system for co-operatives and mutuals:

Birchall, J. (2011). "A 'Member-Owned Business' Approach to the Classification of Co-operatives and Mutuals". *Journal of Co-operative Studies, 44*(2), 4-15.

Atherton, J., Birchall, J., Mayo, E. and Simon, G. (2012) *Practical Tools for Defining Co-operative and Mutual Enterprises*, Manchester: Co-operatives UK.

5 **Mobile Phone Minutes (MPMs) as a currency -** this is not a fiction. Colleagues in Social Enterprise Europe working in Africa say that in some communities goods are priced in mobile phone minutes. A mobile phone app is used to transfer minutes from the customer to the shop keeper.

6 **Co-operative Bank plc -** Warren's confusion is understandable. In 2013, the Co-operative Bank (notionally owned by the customers of the Co-operative Group) was sold off to US hedge funds when a combination of poor trading and new banking regulations left it with a £1.5 billion 'black hole' in its finances. Unlike the Nationwide Building Society which raised such monies from its members, the Co-operative Group ceded control to US hedge funds who had actively organised small investors to oppose the Co-operative Group's plans. These hedge funds then sold on their holding to other hedge funds (one even before a vote of small investors had taken place). After ceding control, the Co-operative Bank plc announced its plans to list on the London Stock Exchange.

In 2014, in separate developments at the Co-operative Group (the former parent company of the bank), a new board adopted norms of the City of London for its corporate governance and broke with 150 years of member control. They changed the constitution so that the Board would have a majority of 'independent' directors. Only 3 of 11 directors are now nominated and elected by the members of the Co-operative Group. The members also adopted a rule that prevents them from changing their own constitution without the Board's approval. Members' voice has been retained through a 100 strong Members Council with a President that monitors the work of the Board.

See ***The Guardian***

"Hedge fund sells up after forcing Co-op to cede control of bank", 28th November 2013

"Co-op members vote to back radical changes", 30th August 2014.

[7] **Co-operative Equity** - in co-operative economics, equity can normally be withdrawn rather than transferred (i.e. sold). New regulations in the Co-operatives and Community Benefit Society's Act 2014 clarify that transfers are allowed, but must be subject to the same due diligence that covers companies.

Snaith, I. (2014) *The Handbook of Co-operative and Community Benefit Society Law,* Manchester: Co-operatives UK.

Brown, J. (2004). *Co-operative Capital: a new approach to investment in co-operatives*. Manchester: Cooperative Action.

[8] **Investors in co-operatives** - there is a latent hostility to 'outside investors' in many co-operatives (particularly worker co-operatives). Internationally, there are many cases of pragmatic co-operation between member-owners and institutional owners to advance the co-operative model. Employee-owned companies can adopt hybrid structures to reconcile staff and institutional investor interests, or manage the shareholdings of outgoing owners while they are transferred to employee owners. See the article/book chapter:

Ridley-Duff, R. (2009). "Co-operative social enterprises: company rules, access to finance and management practice", *Social Enterprise Journal, 5*(1), 50-68.

Ridley-Duff, R. (2012). "New frontiers in democratic self-management", In: McDonnell, D. and MacKnight, E., (eds.) *The Co-operative Model in Practice.* Glasgow, Co-operative Education Trust Scotland, pp. 99-118.

[9] **Better Health -** although this is a fictional company, the idea is not a fiction. I have invited speakers from a UK region in the North West of England to discuss/describe the success of a

social enterprise that built clinics for health providers. It was so successful that the local health authority and construction companies worked together to close it down. The health authority did not want its power to design facilities usurped by a social enterprise. The construction companies did not want to see profits go into a social enterprise (where it could be used only for social objects and not to pay shareholder dividends). Within 5 years, the social enterprise had saved taxpayers £600,000 and was steadily reinvesting in new health facilities.

It was forced to close in 2009, but in 2010 the law changed after a new government was elected. With these changes, social enterprises acquired a *theoretical* power that enabled them to bid for contracts to design and deliver public services. In *practice,* procurement rules set such a high bar that it precluded almost all social enterprises from bidding for contracts.

So - in 2014 - the *Social Economy Alliance* published a manifesto arguing for contracts of a certain type to be delivered only by social enterprises. This manifesto will be used to lobby political parties in the run up to the 2015 election. Already, some larger employee-owned / co-owned businesses have been able to bid successfully for contracts in the health sector. See: http://www.circlepartnership.co.uk/about-circle/our-partnership

10 **Loomio, Co-budget, Crowdfunder, Kickstarter, Zopa, Microgenius, Crowdcube and Funding Circle** - these were all real products/websites at the time of writing. Co-budget was in development, but videos of the prototype are available. All products are internet-based collaborative decision-making, budgeting and investing tools - ideal for a co-operative economy.

See the following:

- Loomio: https://www.loomio.org/
- Co-budgetting: http://vimeo.com/90498374
- Crowdfunder: www.crowdfunder.com / www.crowdfunder.co.uk
- Kickstarter: https://www.kickstarter.com/

- Zopa: http://www.zopa.com/
- Microgenius: http://www.microgenius.org.uk/
- Crowdcube: http://www.crowdcube.com/
- Funding Circle: https://www.fundingcircle.com/

[11] **Members Direct** is a fictional organisation, but the idea is based on **Supporters Direct** which exists. **Supporters Direct** creates strategies for sport fans to buy shares – and in some cases majority control - of the sports clubs they support. In the UK, there are now nearly 200 sports clubs structured this way with some already in professional leagues. Internationally, **Barcelona FC** is probably the best known example of a fan-owned sports club. All top flights German football teams also have to be majority owned by their fans.

Supporters Direct: http://www.supporters-direct.org/

Barcelona FC: http://www.fcbarcelona.com/

[12] **Private and Personal Property** - the documentary *The Corporation* examines how companies ('legal persons') acquired the same legal rights as humans ('natural persons'). The documentary shows how corporations use their legal person rights to deny natural persons the rights originally created for them. To reduce the power of corporations, therefore, 'personal' and 'private' property need to be distinguished and corporate use of 'personal' rights needs to be restricted. See: http://www.thecorporation.com/

[13] **ASBOs** - anti-social behaviour orders became common place in the 1990s for dealing with noisy neighbours and drunken behaviour in town centres. They were also applied to rowdy sports fans. However, the idea of extending ASBOs to anti-social *investment* behaviour is new. This is the legal innovation suggested by this novella.

[14] **Leveson Report** – this report, revised in December 2013, examined phone hacking by newspapers in the UK. It triggered the creation of new bodies for press regulation and ongoing

campaigns to protect all people from unwarranted invasions of privacy. Executives from News International were prosecuted for corrupting people in public office, and five people - including David Cameron's former Director of Communications, Neil Coulson – were jailed.

See: http://www.levesoninquiry.org.uk/

15 **Constabularies (Civil Society and the Police)** – this idea bears a resemblance to the early development of the Metropolitan Police in London. Before 1829, law enforcement was carried out by unpaid constables who were elected by the community. Henry Fielding, an author, allowed his house to be used as a court from 1739 and became a magistrate in 1748. In 1753 he created the Bow Street Runners who worked with justices of the peace to enforce local laws. In 1805, they adopted a uniform and amalgamated with other units to establish a permanent police force.

It was not until 1829 that the Metropolitan Police Act created a civilian (non-military) authority with paid staff who took preventative and enforcement measures.

Source: Metropolitan Police Archives / Old Bailey Online (Wikipedia "History of the Metropolitan Police Service")

16 **Patient Opinion** is a real organisation with over 50 employee owners based in Sheffield, England (see www.patientopinion.org.uk). Employee Opinion and Citizen Opinion are fictional companies that follow the same logic as Patient Opinion in design and purpose. There is, however, a website which enables employees to review their employers (www.glassdoor.co.uk). The reviews are cursory rather than the detailed stories/accounts provided by Patient Opinion. Glassdoor is effectively a consumer information portal whereas Patient Opinion seeks to create a dialogue between itself and health services to improve practice.

17 **Owenite** is a reference to Robert Owen, a well-known reformer of education who pioneered the idea of producer co-operatives at New Lanark in the 1820s. Owen, and the Owenties, were pre-

Rochdale co-operators who started a journal in the 1820s. A self-made industrialist from Wales, he believe that working people were shaped by the conditions in which they lived and worked. By changing those conditions and educating them properly, their nature would change. He took his radical ideas to America and invested much of his fortune developing co-operative communities to test his theories.

Today, there is a World heritage site at New Lanark. His legacy lives on - a group of industrialists are working to create a modern version of Owen's vision. A large plot of land – 2000 acres – have been bought to build Owenstown. Although the local council has rejected the plan, the campaign is now lobbying the Scottish Parliament to overturn the decision.

See: http://owenstown.org/

18 **Social Enterprise Definition** - Sharon uses a definition developed by *Social Enterprise Europe* for international work (www.socialenterprise.co.uk) as updated by the *FairShares Association* (www.fairshares.coop) in mid-2014.

19 **Share Dealing Days** are quite common in employee-owned businesses. Both School Trends (a case study for my PhD) and Gripple (a case study undertaken by one of my PhD students) have a share dealing day each year. On that day, members can trade their shares and – in the case of School Trends – buy and sell shares through an Employee Share Ownership Trust company (ESOT).

20 **Suicides** – whilst studying for my PhD, I found that - contrary to popular belief - suicides amongst men run at more than 4 times the rate of suicides for women up to the age of 44. Office of National Statistics data (1975 – 2000) shows that young men were 3.2 times more likely to commit suicide in 1974 and 4.6 times as likely by 2000. Likelihood of suicide amongst 15 – 44 year old men had risen 76.2% over this 25 year period compared to a 4.2% drop for women of the same age. For a discussion of US data see:

Farrell, W. (1994) *The Myth of Male Power,* Berkley Trade. [21st Anniversary Edition - www.warrenfarrell.com]

[21] **Wealth Creation** – studies at Harvard University have reported that the top 1% of earners took 9% of national income in the 1970s rising to 24% in 2010. Research from Stanford shows that all the increased wealth of the US has gone the highest quintile – there has been a net decrease in wealth for everyone else. So, the people Harold defends are 'wealth creators' for the top 10% and 'wealth destroyers' for the other 90%.

Grusky, D. et al. (2014) *State of the Union: The Poverty and Inequality Report 2014*, Stanford Center on Poverty and Inequality.

Norton, M. I., & Ariely, D. (2011). "Building a better America—One wealth quintile at a time", *Perspectives on Psychological Science*, 6(1), 9-12. [The authors are Harvard Professors]

An animated representation of Norton and Ariely's work is available on YouTube.

[22] **Referenda** are a way of life for citizens in Switzerland, but are extremely rare in the UK. In Switzerland, a petition signed by 100,000 people can trigger a referendum. Wikipedia reports that 11 referenda were held in Switzerland during 2013, and a further 9 during 2014. In the US, state referenda take place on the day of the Presidential elections.

http://en.wikipedia.org/wiki/Swiss_referendums,_2014

[23] **Plebgate** – during 2012 a 'plebgate' scandal took place in the UK after it was alleged that a Tory Chief Whip (Andrew Mitchell) had used this term after getting angry at police who would not let him cycle into Downing Street. However, later, the police officers were sacked for the way they leaked elements of the story to the press. Although Andrew Mitchell continually claimed his words were misrepresented, he now faces a High Court challenge by PC Toby Rowland for not telling the truth about what was said.

See: http://www.bbc.co.uk/news/uk-24548645

[24] **Green Economics** – alone amongst mainstream political parties, the Greens do not equate 'growth' (a rising GDP) with rising

standards of living. For example, widespread use of energy saving devices might lead to falls in GDP, but still increase quality of life.

Bauhardt, C. (2014). "Solutions to the crisis? The Green New Deal, Degrowth, and the Solidarity Economy: Alternatives to the capitalist growth economy from an eco-feminist economics perspective", *Ecological Economics, 102*, 60-68.

[25] **Polanyi's** works are proving popular amongst European social enterprise researchers within the EMES research network. I have also cited his work *The Great Transformation* in two of my publications.

Polyani, K. (1944). *The Great Transformation*. New York: Rinehart.

[26] **Hayek and Friedman** were key influencers of the 'new right' in the 1970s. Hayek famously claimed there would be a 'trickle down' effect if entrepreneurs were left to create more jobs and wealth. By 2008, this theory was in tatters as research established that the bottom 80% of US citizens now owned only 7% of the nation's wealth between them. Hayek's and Friedman's economic theories produced a 'trickle up' of gigantic proportions.

Hayek, F. (1976) *Law, Legislation and Liberty: the Mirage of Social Justice*, London: Routledge and Kegan Paul.

Friedman, M. (2009). *Capitalism and freedom*. University of Chicago Press. [First published 1962]

[27] **Marx and Engels** wrote *The Communist Manifesto* together. Engels is best known for *The Origins of the Family, Private Property and the State* while Marx is best known for *Capital.* There has been a resurgent interest in Marx's works, particularly in Germany, since the financial crash of 2008.

Marx, K., & Engels, F. (2002). *The Communist Manifesto*. Penguin. [First published 1848].

Engels, F. (2010). *The Origin of the Family, Private Property and the State*. Penguin UK. [First published 1884]

[28] **Vets School** – this was a BBC series following trainee vets through their studies. It became so popular that it spawned a follow up series called **Vets in Practice**.

[29] **The Secret Millionaire** – there were US and UK versions of this programme. Millionaires go under cover in charities to see how they work and then surprise the charity workers at the end of the programme by donating (substantially) to their finances.

[30] **Spedan Lewis, John** was an advocate of producer cooperation, but resisted being labelled a communist. He called JLP an 'industrial democracy'. In the book *Fairer Shares* he positioned employee ownership as 'perhaps the only alternative to communism' based on three core principles: 1) sharing gains; 2) sharing information, and; 3) sharing power.

Lewis, J. S. (1954). *Fairer Shares: A Possible Advance in Civilisation and Perhaps the Only Alternative to Communism*. Staples Press.

[31] **Scotland** narrowly voted against independence (45% v 55%) in September 2014. The Scottish Nationalist leader Alex Salmond stated that the issue was closed for that generation, but the local papers suggested it could be earlier if the UK government failed to deliver on promises made during the referendum.

[32] **FairShares Model** – the first formalised description of the FairShares Model was published by myself, Cliff Southcombe and Nicci Dickins in February 2013. Version 2.0 was released on 1st July 2014 at the first conference of the FairShares Association. It draws on 30 years of work to create model rules for multi-stakeholder co-operation under company and co-operative law.

Ridley-Duff, R., Bull, M. (2013) "The FairShares Model: a communitarian pluralist approach to constituting social enterprises", in *ISBE Conference 2013*, Cardiff City Hall, 12th-13th November.

Ridley-Duff, R. (2014) *The Case for a FairShares Model of Enterprise*, Sheffield: FairShares Association, https://www.fairshares-association.com/wordpress/the-case-for-fairshares/

Ridley-Duff, R. (2014) *FairShares Model V2.0: a new model for self-governing social enterprises operating under Association, Company and Co-operative Law*, Sheffield: FairShares Association, http://shura.shu.ac.uk/8470/

[33] **Working Peoples Bank** – This is a translation of the name of the credit union in the Basque region of Spain that working people supported to provide the capital for the Mondragon Co-operatives (Caja Laboral Popular Cooperativa de Crédito). By 1980, 300,000 local people had accounts. By 2000, 24,000 of the 28,000 people in the town of Mondragon had an investment in one or more of the town's co-operatives.

See http://en.wikipedia.org/wiki/Caja_Laboral

[34] **Ellerman, David** was the speech writer for Joseph Stiglitz at the World Bank. His book *The Democratic Firm* unambiguously attributes responsibility for 'added value' to the workforce. He argues that capital cannot add value, only be the factor that enables the purchase of means of production. Added value is created by the workforce which – under a Labour Theory of Property – makes it the rightful owners of any value added.

Ellerman, D. (1990). *The Democratic Worker-Owned Firm: A New Model for the East and for the West,* London: Hyman.

[35] **Patterson, John** wrote papers in response to the Corporate Law Review 2003 showing that in the event of a company closure, the workforce members suffer - on average - a 25% reduction in income. When multiplied by the number of workforce members affected, the 'risk capital' of the workforce was as great (or greater) than the risk capital of institutional investors. On this basis, workers should be entitled to equity in the firm equal or exceeding the equity of external investors because they share the risk equally.

Paterson, JB. (2003). 'The Company Law Review in the UK and the Question of Scope: Theoretical Concerns, Practical Constraints and Possible New Directions'. in J Lenoble & R Cobbaut (eds), *Corporate Governance: An Institutional Approach.* Kluwer Law International, The Hague, Netherlands, pp. 141-184.

[36] **Mutuals / Co-operative Financial Institutions** – ICMIF reported that the market share of co-operative and mutual institutions in European financial services rose from 22.6% in 2007 to 28.1% in 2011. The assets of UK credit unions doubled in the 5 years to 2010.

[37] **Zopa** is a real internet-based mutual savings organisation. I have borrowed from it to buy a car, and also lent money through it to over 200 small borrowers. Zopa take savers money, divide it up into small amounts (£10 - £20) and lends it to borrowers. At the time of writing, Zopa UK had over 57,000 members who lent over half a billion pounds directly to borrowers. The average return was 5.2% (double the rate most high street banks were offering to savers at the time). See http://www.zopa.com/.

[38] **The Grameen Bank** is a real bank in Bangladesh started by Nobel Prize Winner Muhammad Yunus. Each Grameen branch has 30 people comprising six groups of five who form lending circles. Members in the circle can only borrow if repayments by other members are up to date creating peer-pressure that reduces debt. Only rural people with less than ½ an acre of land (85% women) were eligible for membership. Initially the government put in the money, but over time ownership was transferred to the members. Grameen's microfinance model has been replicated in many parts of the world, including Glasgow, Scotland, where there is a Yunus Centre for Social Business (Glasgow Caledonian University).

Jain, P. S. (1996). "Managing credit for the rural poor: lessons from the Grameen Bank", *World Development*, 24(1), 79-89.

Yunus, M. (2007). *Creating a World Without Poverty: Social Business and the Future of Capitalism*. PublicAffairs.

[39] **Piketty, Thomas** – a French economist who published a widely debated work called *Capital in the 21st Century* in 2013. His research suggested that parliamentary democracy and free market competition did not narrow the wealth gap between rich and poor. Only social democratic states had been effective at closing the wealth gap. Elsewhere (except in times of war) the rich always find ways to allocate themselves a disproportionately large share of any wealth produced.

Piketty, T. (2013). *Capital in the Twenty-first Century.* Harvard University Press.

[40] **Creative Commons** is a modern licensing system designed for creative people to share public rights in their works (see https://creativecommons.org/). It has been adopted by many notable institutions, including the World Bank (for all its publications).

[41] **FairShares Association** - formed by six people in February 2013 and held its first conference on 1st July 2014. The first social enterprise network in Europe to bid for EU money to develop a national FairShares project was SLAP ('waterfall' in Croatian). This Association for Creative Development bid for 965, 000 € with Social Enterprise Europe in August 2014.

[42] **Qualifying Contributions** for shares. Whilst there are some mechanisms for 'free shares' in employee-owned businesses, and many 'employee share schemes', the principle of allocating shares for investments of labour is usually overshadowed by share allocations for entrepreneurial effort or financial investment. For example, when Royal Mail was sold off in 2013, 90% of shares were given to institutional investors and only 10% to the workforce.

[43] **Poverty Trap** – this term was applied frequently to any welfare system where taking a job left a person on a low income worse off. If benefits are withdrawn more quickly than earnings rise, a low income household is worse off working. This was (is) the poverty trap that acts as a disincentive to seeking paid employment.

[44] **Stanford and Harvard Research** – the works referred to are:

Grusky, D. et al. (2014) *State of the Union: The Poverty and Inequality Report 2014*, Stanford Center on Poverty and Inequality.

Norton, M. I., & Ariely, D. (2011). Building a better America—One wealth quintile at a time. *Perspectives on Psychological Science*, *6*(1), 9-12. [Harvard Professors]

[45] **Judges Supporting FairShares** - the scene in which Judge Patricia shows support for FairShares is based on fact not fiction. Social Enterprise Europe has been undertaking a project in Nigeria where judges are actively considering use of FairShares as a legal structure for local courts. This would put the running of the courts into the hands of the judges and citizens and prevent much of the corruption that currently occurs.

Bibliography

Bauhardt, C. (2014). "Solutions to the crisis? The Green New Deal, Degrowth, and the Solidarity Economy: Alternatives to the capitalist growth economy from an eco-feminist economics perspective", *Ecological Economics, 102*, 60-68.

Birchall, J. (2011). "A 'Member-Owned Business' Approach to the Classification of Co-operatives and Mutuals". *Journal of Co-operative Studies, 44*(2), 4-15.

Brown, J. (2004). *Co-operative Capital–A new approach to investment in co-operatives.* Manchester: Cooperative Action.

Ellerman, D. (1990). *The Democratic Worker-Owned Firm: A New Model for the East and for the West,* London: Hyman.

Engels, F. (2010). *The Origin of the Family, Private Property and the State.* Penguin UK. [First published 1884]

Farrell, W. (1994) *The Myth of Male Power,* Berkley Trade. [21st Anniversary Edition available from www.warrenfarrell.com]

Friedman, M. (2009). *Capitalism and freedom.* University of Chicago Press. [First published 1962]

Grusky, D. et al. (2014) *State of the Union: The Poverty and Inequality Report 2014,* Stanford Center on Poverty and Inequality.

Hayek, F. (1976) *Law, Legislation and Liberty: the Mirage of Social Justice,* London: Routledge and Kegan Paul.

Jain, P. S. (1996). "Managing credit for the rural poor: lessons from the Grameen Bank", *World Development, 24*(1), 79-89.

Lewis, J. S. (1954). *Fairer Shares: A Possible Advance in Civilisation and Perhaps the Only Alternative to Communism.* Staples Press.

Marx, K., & Engels, F. (2002). *The Communist Manifesto.* Penguin. [First published 1848].

Norton, M. I., & Ariely, D. (2011). Building a better America—One wealth quintile at a time. *Perspectives on Psychological Science, 6*(1), 9-12. [Harvard Professors]

Paterson, JB. (2003). 'The Company Law Review in the UK and the Question of Scope: Theoretical Concerns, Practical Constraints and Possible New Directions'. in J Lenoble & R Cobbaut (eds), *Corporate Governance: An Institutional Approach.* Kluwer Law International, The Hague, Netherlands, pp. 141-184.

Piketty, T. (2013). *Capital in the Twenty-first Century.* Harvard University Press.

Polyani, K. (1944). *The Great Transformation.* New York: Rinehart.

Ridley-Duff, R., & Bennett, A. (2011). "Towards mediation: developing a theoretical framework to understand alternative dispute resolution", *Industrial Relations Journal, 42*(2), 106-123.

Ridley-Duff, R. and Bull, M. (2015) *Understanding Social Enterprise: Theory and Practice,* 2nd Edition, London: Sage Publications, forthcoming.

Ridley-Duff, R. (2009). "Co-operative social enterprises: company rules, access to finance and management practice", *Social Enterprise Journal, 5*(1), 50-68.

Ridley-Duff, R. (2012). "New frontiers in democratic self-management", In: McDonnell, D. and MacKnight, E., (eds.) *The Co-operative Model in Practice.* Glasgow, Co-operative Education Trust Scotland, pp. 99-118.

Ridley-Duff, R., Bull, M. (2013) "The FairShares Model: a communitarian pluralist approach to constituting social enterprises", in *ISBE Conference 2013,* Cardiff City Hall, 12th-13th November.

Ridley-Duff, R. *The Case for a FairShares Model of Enterprise,* Sheffield: FairShares Association, https://www.fairshares-association.com/wordpress/the-case-for-fairshares/

Ridley-Duff, R. (2014) *FairShares Model V2.0: a new model for self-governing social enterprises operating under Association, Company and Co-operative Law,* Sheffield: FairShares Association, http://shura.shu.ac.uk/8470/

Snaith, I. (2014) *The Handbook of Co-operative and Community Benefit Society Law,* Manchester: Co-operatives UK.

Yunus, M. (2007). *Creating a World Without Poverty: Social Business and the Future of Capitalism.* PublicAffairs.

Rory Ridley-Duff

Fast forward to 2032. In a co-operative world full of social enterprises, the BBC hires a new quartet of Dragons…

Warren is an entrepreneur who has successfully amassed billions. Unfortunately, since receiving an ASBO for anti-social investing, he has been banned from starting any new ventures. Then he receives a call from Sharon - an ambitious producer at the BBC – to ask if he would like to put his unemployed capital back to work on a new game show. Should he accept?

Dr Rory Ridley-Duff is Reader in Co-operative and Social Enterprise at Sheffield Business School, a director of Social Enterprise Europe Ltd, and is a co-founder of the FairShares Association. He is an editorial board member of the Social Enterprise Journal and co-opted board member of the UK Society for Co-operative Studies. His book, *Understanding Social Enterprise: Theory and Practice* (co-authored with Mike Bull) is used by co-operative and social enterprise educators on four continents.

He previous books include:

- **Silent Revolution**: creating and managing social enterprises
- **False Accusation** (previously published as *Friends or Lovers*)
- **Emotion, Seduction and Intimacy**: alternative perspectives on human behaviour
- **Understanding Social Enterprise**: theory and practice

This novella was started during the United Nations **International Year of Cooperatives in 2012** and was completed after hosting the inaugural conference of the FairShares Association at Sheffield Business School, England in 2014.

CPSIA information can be obtained at www.ICGtesting.com
Printed in the USA
LVOW07s1938140515

438535LV00001B/18/P